Francis O Davenport

On a Man-of-War

A series of naval sketches

Francis O Davenport

On a Man-of-War
A series of naval sketches

ISBN/EAN: 9783744742917

Printed in Europe, USA, Canada, Australia, Japan

Cover: Foto ©Andreas Hilbeck / pixelio.de

More available books at **www.hansebooks.com**

U. S. S. F. FRANKLIN.

On A Man-of-War.

A

Series of Naval Sketches.

BY

Francis O Davenport.

LIEUT. COMMANDER U. S. NAVY.

> How gloriously her gallant course she goes!
> Her white wings flying—never from her foes
> She walks the water like a thing of life,
> And seems to dare the elements to strife.
> Who would not brave the battle-fire—the wreck—
> To move the monarch of her peopled deck?
>
> BYRON: *Corsair*

DETROIT:
R. B. SMITH & CO.,
1878.

Stereotyped and Printed
by the
Detroit Free Press Co.

PREFACE.

— ••• —

In submitting this book, or collection of letters, to the public, I desire to preface it with some appropriate remarks.

I was, truly and honestly, asked to write some letters descriptive of life on a man-of-war, narratives of real facts and incidents in my naval career.

With some diffidence—this is also true—I sent material for three or four letters to the office of the *Detroit Free Press*, with directions to curtail, amend or suppress, as the superior editorial mind should think proper. To my surprise and pleasure, the letters appeared in full, without correction or abbreviation.

Upon the appearance of these letters from time to time, in the Sunday paper, I was overwhelmed with compliments from my friends, expressing the hope that the letters would be continued. Five cents for a paper is very little, I know, and the sacrifice is still less when you borrow the paper. I shall, therefore, watch with considerable anxiety, to see if the interested readers of my single articles will stand the test of paying one dollar and a half for the entire series combined.

If my readers—*my* readers sounds good—take as much

pleasure in reading these letters as I have taken in reviving these old reminiscences, I shall feel amply repaid (this, of course, does *not* include the price of the book, one dollar and a half, bound in calf).

As this volume is instructive, written "to meet a long felt want," I would say that none should be without a copy of it. To that end, I respectfully suggest to *my* readers—that is, the purchasers of my book—not to lend it, but to advise would-be borrowers that it would be pure madness for any one to take any chance of being without this valuable work.

A SCRAP FROM THE U. S. NAVAL ACADEMY.

— •◦• —

Now list, ye winds, while I repeat
A parting signal to the fleet.
  Whose station is at home:
Then waft a sea-boy's simple prayer,
And be it oft remembered there
  While other climes I roam.

Farewell to Father, reverend hulk,
Who, spite of metal, spite of bulk,
  Must soon his cable slip.
But, e'er he's broken ground, I'll try
The flag of gratitude to fly,
  In duty to the ship.

Farewell to Mother, first-class she,
Who launched me on life's troubled sea,
  And rigged me fore and aft:
May Heaven, to her, her timbers spare,
And keep her hull in good repair,
  To tow the smaller craft.

Farewell to Sister, lovely yacht,
But whether she'll be spliced or not,
   I cannot now foresee;
But may some craft a tender prove,
Well found in stores of youth and love,
   To take her under lee.

Farewell to Jack, the jolly boat,
And all the little craft afloat
   In home's delightful bay;
When they arrive at sailing age,
Some trusty pilot may engage,
   To get them under weigh.

Farewell to all on life's wide main,
We ne'er perchance may meet again,
   Thro'. stress of stormy weather;
Till, summoned by the Board above,
We'll anchor in the Port of Love,
   And all be moored together.

ON A MAN-OF-WAR.

"The seaman, safe on shore, with joy doth tell
What cruel dangers him at sea befell."

LETTER I.

DETAILS OF FITTING OUT A SHIP FOR A CRUISE — THE OFFICERS AND CREW—THE ARMAMENT—THE EVOLUTIONS—A CALL TO THE MAINMAST—THE WATCHES—THE BOATS' CREWS—IN COMMISSION—THE LOG.

My Dear Fellow—You have often asked me to give you some idea of the general routine on board an American man-of-war, and I know of no better way than to jot down my actual experience in the fitting out of a ship from a navy yard.

On the 9th of June I was suddenly detached from the United States Naval Academy by the following order :

You are hereby detached from the Naval Academy, and you will proceed to Boston, Massachusetts, without delay, and report to Rear Admiral Stringham for duty on board the U. S. S. ———, second rate.

I am very respectfully your obedient servant,

GIDEON WELLES,
Secretary of the Navy.

To Lieut. ———, United States Navy.

I arrived at the navy yard and presented myself at the commandant's office at 10 A. M. to report, and being provided by the friendly clerk in the office with

the objectionable uniform cap, invented by one of
the old Admirals, and only worn when one was afraid
not to wear it, I entered the Admiral's sanctum to
introduce myself and get his indorsement on my
orders that I had so reported.

You see, my dear boy, that the paymaster pays
according to your "orders," and until I reported I
was on "leave" pay, whereas as soon as I reported I
became entitled to "other duty" pay, which is twenty
per cent higher. As soon as the ship is put in commission the officers are entitled to "sea pay," which
is still higher.

After reporting I went at once to the ship, which
was moored at the wharf and filled with carpenters
and riggers busily engaged fitting the ship for sea.
The ship is in the hands of the navy yard officers
until she is put in commission and is turned over to
the commanding officer of the ship in the presence of
his officers and crew, at that time complete and ready
for sea. Until this ceremony takes place the officers
of the ship have no authority on board, the employés
of the yard getting their orders from the officers
attached to the navy yard only, and not from the
officers of the ship.

The various officers, on reporting for duty to the
commander, are, however, directed to report on board
daily, and watch that their various departments are

being properly supplied by the authorities of the yard.

The first lieutenant or executive officer, has a general superintendence, and conveys the wishes of the commander of the vessel to the junior officers. The second lieutenant, who is ordnance officer and navigator, assisted by the gunner, and by his signal quartermaster, looks after the storage of the shell rooms, shot lockers and the various chronometers, compasses, sextants, lead lines, etc., belonging to the navigator.

A certain allowance of seamen, ordinary seamen, landsmen and boys is detailed from the receiving ship as a crew for the vessel fitting out, and every officer, who is interested, visits the receiving ship to find out if there is some particular one that he wants, and works wires as best he can to get his choice included in the list finally detailed to the ship.

The captain is on the lookout for a good cook and steward; so also is the caterer of the ward room mess, the steerage mess, and the warrant officers' mess; and as the pay is higher in the order mentioned, the quality is generally the same.

When the ship is quite ready the crew is sent on board, and all hands being assembled on the quarter deck the flag is hoisted at the peak and the pennant to the main truck, and the ship formally turned over to its commander by the commandant of the yard, and the ship is in "commission."

The executive officer at once organizes the crew, dividing the men into two watches—starboard and port watch, so many men as forecastlemen, foretopmen, maintopmen, mizzentopmen and afterguards.

The forecastlemen do duty from the foremast forward; the foretopmen, aloft and on port side from foremast to mainmast; the maintopmen, aloft and on starboard side from foremast to mainmast; mizzentopmen, aloft and on port side from mainmast aft; and afterguards on starboard side aft.

A foretopman would look with pitying contempt on a young officer who directed him to "squilgee down" in the starboard gangway, and would call one of the maintopmen to look out for his own part of the ship. One of our admirals was ordered out to take command of the Mediterranean squadron, and, upon coming on board the flagship, was met at the gangway by an old classmate (the one he was to relieve) with the salutation, "Hallo, old fellow, how are you?" and observing that the Admiral had carefully combed his back hair forward up and over to cover the bald top of his head, added, "Well, that's the first time I ever saw afterguard doing foretop duty."

The executive officer selects from the crew the

petty officers as allowed by the allowance book. I had fifty to choose. One master at arms, who is chief of police, and in charge of berth deck; two ship's corporals, aids to master at arms; four coxswains; two captains of the forecastle; two captains of the foretop; two captains of the maintop, mizzen and afterguard; two boatswain's mates, one gunner's mate, four quarter gunners, etc. When the list is made out the captain approves and directs the paymaster to take them up on his books according to the pay of their respective offices. A seaman gets $18 a month and his ration, while the petty officers get $20, $24 and even $30, and in steamers the machinists get, I think, $76.50 a month.

The crew is then stationed for every evolution, and each man can find his station by his hammock number, displayed in some suitable place framed for their inspection. As each man has to be stationed for "getting under weigh," "bringing ship to an anchor," "tacking ship," "wearing ship," "loosing and furling," "reefing topsails," "in and out boats," "up and down topgallant and royal yards," etc., it is no small piece of work to watch and station a crew of 500 men. Then the crew has to be "quartered," or stationed at the guns. Our ship had twenty-two guns on the gun deck—ten nine-inch forming the first division, in charge of the third lieutenant, and twelve long thirty-two's, forming the second division, in charge of the fourth lieutenant; eight thirty-two's on the quarter deck, four thirty-two's forward, with a hundred-pounder rifled Parrot on the forecastle and another aft.

The navigator had charge of the powder division, passing the different cylinders or cartridges for the guns of the various calibers.

The captain is stationed where he chooses, generally on the bridge, and the executive by his side, or where he can see the best and make himself heard.

I then assigned the different crews to the eight boats. This is a very nice operation, as you want the best men, who generally pull the best oar, and if you take too many from one part of the ship you are soon notified that Brown, the "captain of the forecastle," is at the mast and wishes to speak to the first lieutenant. (The mainmast is the tribunal of justice on board a man-of-war, and a man at the mast must be attended to.)

"If you please, sir, we didn't have but two men, starboard watch, this morning to wash decks."

"Two! Why not?"

"Why, there's four gigsmen, and they was to sleep in till six bells" (the captain was out till one o'clock), "and there was one in the dingey (market boat), and Smith he's cook of the mess, Flattery is on the list (sick list), and Tom Scott didn't come off last night in the ten o'clock boat. I wish, sir, you'd give us a man for sweeper, sir. That Jones, sir, ain't fit for captain of the head, sir."

If I promised him a man from the main top you can depend upon it I heard from the "captain of the maintop" right away.

The captains of the tops and coxswains of boats are petty tyrants and exact the most implicit obedience from their inferiors.

The flag is hoisted at 8 A. M. in summer and at 9 A. M. in winter at the peak of the spanker, and should always be taut or close up to the peak. The pennant should never be hauled down, as it is the designating mark of a ship in commission, and when the long day pennant is changed at sunset for the short night pennant the latter is sent up in a ball and the stop broken as the other comes down. I have heard an irascible old captain "holler" at a quartermaster for neglecting this ceremony, saying, "D—n your eyes, do you want to put the ship out of commission, sir?" The Union Jack, white stars on a blue field, is hoisted on a flag-staff stepped on the bowsprit cap, and is displayed at the same time with the "colors," and like them hauled down at sunset. During a funeral ceremony the colors are half-masted or lowered about one-third the way down, and I heard the captain one day, coming on board and observing the halliards slacked down about *two inches* go for the officer of the deck with the sarcastic question,

" Anybody dead, sir ?"

Whereupon the officer of the deck turned hastily to the quartermaster with:

" Get a pull of those peak halliards there."

After a ship is put in commission the watches are at once organized, the starboard watch being on four hours and then the port watch, the watch from 4 to 8 P. M. being subdivided into the dog watches from 4 to 6 and 6 to 8 in order to produce rotation, otherwise one watch would have the "eight hours out," 8 P. M. to 12 and 4 to 8 A. M., and the other the "mid watch," 12 to 4 A. M., every night. In harbor an "anchor watch" only is kept, being "one or two men from each part of the ship," as may be directed by the captain.

There are generally four watch officers, lieutenants, masters, ensigns and even midshipmen, according to the size of the ship, the number of officers and the liberality of the commander in giving the youngsters a chance to work ship and stand a watch.

In large ships the midshipmen go in charge of boats, carry messages to other ships, stand a watch on the forecastle at sea, attend to heaving the log, taking the temperature and making the entries on the log slate of barometer, direction of wind, state of weather, the proportion of sky clear, etc.

The officer of the deck is an important personage. He gives every order that is given on deck, directed, of course, by the captain or first lieutenant. He is responsible for the cleanliness of the ship, that the routine is carried on and the general duty during his four hours' watch. He makes and takes in sail, sends away boats and directs the disposition of them on their return, and everybody goes to the officer of the deck for everything. At the end of his watch he writes up his remarks opposite the tabular statement written up by the midshipman somewhat as follows:

At Sea, August 24th, 1870.

"Commenced clear and pleasant with light southerly breezes, sky cirro cumulus, ship under plain sail. At 2.30 A. M. wind veered to northward and eastward, overcast and cloudy, with occasional squalls; took in royals, hauled down flying jib. At three single reefed topsails and changed course to northwest. F. L. W."

The log slate is copied into the log book and signed by the officer every day. The log book also shows how many sticks of wood were served out to the cooks and also how many gallons of water, with the balance on hand. The engineer's log shows how many pounds of coal have been burned and how much

is left on hand.   We had tanks carrying 40,000 gallons of water, and I drank some of the water when
we returned to Boston one year after it had been put
in, and it was sweet and pure.

LETTER II.

HOW A VESSEL GETS UNDER WEIGH—ALL HANDS LOOSE
SAIL.—ALOFT SAIL LOOSERS—BRINGING THE SHIP
TO ANCHOR.

In my last letter I explained substantially the fitting out of a man-of-war from the navy yard, so now, if you are interested, I will endeaver to give you some idea of the routine of a ship in commission.

The next morning after the ceremony of putting the ship in commission, the captain gave me orders to get the ship under weigh, under sail at 2 P. M. and go down the harbor to an anchorage. Of course I was nervous. I was only twenty-two years old, and felt that there were some things about a ship that I did not know; besides, when I stood upon the bridge, I felt so small and the ship looked so infernal long, that I determined at once that the only way to run the ship at all was to claim the privilege of doing all the talking myself. Even on shore, you know, there is a general tendency for every one to suggest how to do it; "they all do it."

In one of Marryat's stories, he describes the getting under weigh of a small schooner, officered by some immense men, where Lieut. B., leveling a long trumpet at the officer of the forecastle, hailed him in pon-

derous tones: "Are you ready, sir?" and was answered
in a deafening shout of "Aye, aye, sir," by that
doughty officer, who at the same time was so close to
him that he nearly blew him off his feet. But here I
had a clear space of about 175 feet to "holler" in,
and if the boats'n's mates whistled and people shouted
as I had heard them do on some other ships, I knew
that I would stand no chance of making myself heard
at all.

I had watched, quartered, and stationed the ship's
crew for everything, but still wondered if I had not
forgotten something. Perhaps when I gave the
order to "frow de ank," de ank might have no
rope to it. The experience of a classmate of mine
did not reassure me, for under precisely similar cir-
cumstances when he gave the order, "Aloft, sail-loosers," he said every mother's son of 'em went aloft,
and he found he had forgotten to station any men at
the clew-jiggers and buntlines on deck, so he had to
call them down and start anew.

Well! all the navy yard people, including some
rather pretty girls, came down to see the S——— get
under weigh; so I marched into the cabin, and swal-
lowing a lump in my throat I said boldly:

"I will get under weigh, sir, if you please."

The captain smiled a little and said, "Certainly,
Mr. ———, whenever you are ready."

So, having no other excuse for delay, I said to the officer of the deck:

"Well, sir, I will relieve you; we will get under weigh."

As we were fast to the wharf, there was no anchor to raise, so I sent a messenger boy to the boatswain, "All hands loose sail," and soon I heard his pipe followed by a second from his mate and third from another mate, and then altogether rising higher and higher and falling, this twice repeated and then the hoarse cry, "Loose sail," "loose sail," "loose sail." I could hear the master at arms on the berth deck: "Look alive there now, tumble up there, on deck there everybody; loose sail"—until I thought I had lost all the sail I wanted to. The men all quickly went, each to the place assigned him, the officers all took their stations, one on the forecastle, one in each gangway and one aft, all curiously looking up to see how the executive would work ship. I felt a little relieved to see that they all seemed to be about where I had seen them in other ships, when I was a junior, and I hoped that I had made no mistakes; and with the feeling that I should not be surprised if the mainmast with all its heavy rigging should suddenly tumble overboard, I put up my trumpet and gave my first order on that eventful cruise:

"Aloft, sail-loosers. Man the boom tricing lines."

And then, with a caution to the men to keep in the slings of the yard until ordered out:

"Trice up — lay out and loose. Man the topsail sheets and halliards—let fall; sheet home, down booms, lay down from aloft. Hoist away the topsails."

The shrill whistle of the boatswains' mates and the prompt obedience to my orders soon restored my confidence, and as we let go our lines and hoisted jib, the old frigate payed off from the wharf and stood beautifully down the harbor, the band playing and friends waving and cheering on the wharf. I was so delighted that at a nod from the captain I gave the order:

"Stand by to man the port rigging and give three cheers. Lay up—cheer—lay down."

So you see that even when we cheer on board ship we have to do it by rule.

We sailed down the harbor with a fair wind, under topsails, jib and spanker until near where we intended to anchor. Then the word was passed with the same ceremony, and whistling "Bring ship to anchor," the men went to their stations. The two men who were to let go the 7,000 pound anchor looked to see if the trip stoppers were all ready; the compressers were hove back to allow the chain to run freely from the chain lockers; the topsail clews were stoppered and the sheets unhooked, and the order given: "Man the topsail, clew jiggers and buntlines; jib downhaul; hands by the sheets and halliards; haul taut; shorten sail."

Up went the clew jiggers, down came the heavy yards on to the caps, quick hands squaring the yards as they came down, down went the helm, and as soon as she lost headway came the order:

"Stand clear of the starboard chain—let go the starboard anchor."

And the ship was riding quietly head to wind, and I was able to "pipe down" and turn the deck over to the regular officer of the watch, to clear up the gear and go to supper.

LETTER III.

At daylight the next morning "all hands were
called," hammocks piped up, lashed neatly and stowed
in the hammock nettings which run round the rail of
the ship, protected from the weather by painted can-
vass hammock cloths, hauled over when the hammocks are all in, and stopped down securely. The
market boat was sent ashore with the various stew-
ards of the different messes, and the order passed to
"wash decks." At 7.15 A. M. the decks were thoroughly cleaned and the ship scrubbed inside and out.
The mess cloths were then spread, and at seven bells
(7.30 A. M.) "piped to breakfast." I then relieved the
officer of the deck to dress, so that when the officer
of the forenoon watch came on at 8.30, having finished breakfast, the other would be able to sit down
to his own, and not delay the ward room boys, making them late to "quarters."

At this time the executive officer receives the reports of the gunner, carpenter, boatswain and sailmaker, all warrant officers drawing pay at from

$1,200 to $1,800 per annum. The gunner reports "the battery secure," and suggests work for the day in his department; the carpenter asks which of the numerous things he shall do first (he has two mates and never catches up with his work during the cruise); there's a hole stove in the second cutter, the garboard streak of the launch wants calking, one of the gigs-men broke an oar and he must cut over one to fit, etc.; the sailmaker reports a chafe in the maintopsail and asks if he can have it unbent and sent down, and reluctantly admits that it *might* be repaired aloft; the boatswain reports that he has been over the ship from the end of the flying jibboom to the tip of the spanker, that all is in order, only a few new ratlines wanted in the topmast rigging, a little chafe in the eyes of the rigging, foremast head, and, if you give him time, he'll make a list that would take three months to complete.

Five minutes before 8 A. M. eight bells is reported to the commander, who may direct that the topgallant and royal yards be crossed, or sails loosed, or some similar evolution be executed with the hoisting of the colors at 8 A. M. If yards are to be crossed "all hands are called," the yards sent up, and at the third roll of the drum the yards swing across, the colors rise to the peak, the pennant changes from short to long pennant, the Jack is hoisted forward at bowsprit cap, the bell strikes eight times, the band plays, the boats to be used during the day are lowered from the davits, and all at once you can imagine a Babel of sounds, but in a well disciplined ship there is no confusion, and comparatively little noise, beyond the shrill whistles of the boatswain and mates, which, by their modulations, indicate " lower away," " hoist," " belay," and " veer," so that orders by voice are not actually necessary.

Sometimes in addition to all the above, sails are loosed, and it tasks an officer to the utmost to see that all goes on well and at once.

At 9.30 the drum beats to quarters, whereupon *every man* repairs to his station at the gun, or particular place assigned him. The officer of the division inspects his division with their arms and accoutrements to see if they are clean and tidy, and that the "bright work" is properly burnished for inspection, reporting the condition to the executive officer, who, in turn, reports to the commander. If that officer expresses his desire to inspect the ship he walks past the various divisions, who salute with the weapons with which they are armed, the powder boys solemnly bringing the priming wires, which they have to clean, to a " present; " and, accompanied by the executive officer, peers into every nook and corner, interspersing the general denunciation with an occasional word of commendation, or *vice versa*.

When Admiral Porter and others inspected this same ship they crawled into the magazines and visited all the store-rooms, and asked me suddenly:

" What hatch is this, sir?"

" The block room, sir."

" Please open it."

When the hatch was taken off, and the combings appeared clean and whitewashed, they winked at each other, and had another obscure one lifted to see if there was any neglect.

I have heard of an austere first lieutenant who was seen to lift one of the shell boxes from its rack on the gun-deck and mark it with his lead-pencil before replacing it, " to see if those negligent rascals would scour it out when they holystoned decks."

After " quarters " there is generally an exercise at great guns, boats, yards and sails, manual of arms, broadswords, howitzer drill, or something of the kind, after which the ten o'clock boat is called away, and those who have permission go ashore, the boat shoving off at the stroke of the bell by order of the officer of the deck, so that those who are not on hand lose their passage and cannot get another boat until 1 P. M.

During the forenoon the work of the ship occupies

every man on board, the executive officer is busy in
consultation with his staff of workmen as before described, the various orders being executed according
to rule and system.

For example, the gunner at 7.30 gets permission of
the executive officer to scrape and relacquer No. 2 gun,
first division. When ready, about 10.30 a. m. he goes
to the officer of the deck and states his authority, the
latter sends a messenger boy to the officer of the first
division, who comes up and requests that the officer
of the deck will have No. 2 gun's crew called to quarters, upon this the gun and crew are turned over to
the gunner to do as he desires. When he has finished
what he wished to do, he secures the gun and reports
the fact to the officer of the deck.

At seven bells (11.30 A. M.), all work ceases, sweepers are piped and "a clean sweep down fore and aft"
ordered; the mess cloths are spread, the ship's cook
brings a sample of the bean soup or the boiled fresh
or salt beef to the mast for inspection, and if ap-
proved he is ordered to "serve it out." At noon the
officer of the deck reports to the captain—"12 o'clock,
sir"—and is ordered to "make it so." Eight bells is
struck and the boatswain and mates pipe to dinner.
If at sea the navigator comes up before 12 to take
observation for latitude, and if in port he takes—a
drink instead.

An Irishman happening to hear the officer of the deck send the orderly to report twelve o'clock to the captain, at once remarked, "Bedad I'd like to be a captain; all he has to do is just to sit in the cabin and they say, 'Eight bells, sir,' and he says, 'Strike it,' says he."

At one P. M. the "hands are turned to," and the 1 o'clock boat sent ashore; work goes on as before until 3.30 P. M., when the decks are swept, and supper piped at 4 P. M. While the crew are at meals a red "meal pennant" is displayed at the mizzen truck or at the crossjack yard arm to warn outsiders that the men are not to be disturbed.

At "sunset" the evening boat returns, the colors are hauled down, with beat of drum and pipe, and the crew are called to evening quarters, which is simply a muster to see if everybody is accounted for.

About six bells (7 P. M.), hammocks are piped. "All hands stand by your hammocks:" the men stand in line abreast of the netting where their hammocks are stowed, and at the order "lay up" and "uncover" the men detailed as hammock stowers swing themselves up and throw back the cloths; "pipe down" is followed by the cries of the eight stowers calling the numbers, "16," "8," "44," etc., and "13," "17," "93," etc., odd numbers being in starboard watch, even numbers port watch, and stowed accordingly.

I fear to weary you by too much detail, and if I become tedious you must warn me. I simply endeavor to show you that absolutely nothing is done on board a man-of-war except by order, and the watchful care and supervision of the officers of a ship are exercised constantly, or the ship becomes uninhabitable.

For example, at certain hours only, the men are allowed to go to their bags, which contain their clothing and which are stowed on the berth deck, under the supervision of the master-at-arms. Were it not for this, thievery would be more prevalent than it is, and the first lieutenant would be kept constantly employed as a detective to punish offenders.

One day the officer of the deck sent me word "that there was a man at the mast." Upon investigation I found that some one had stolen his shirt—"a bran new shirt, sir, with my ship's number marked on back of collar, sir, according to regulation, sir."

I at once turned to the master-at-arms and said "Send William Trusty here."

Trusty had once been a ward room boy, and while hovering round the paymaster, who was writing with the safe open behind him, he had possessed himself of two twenty-dollar greenbacks. He might as well have stolen an elephant, for on the blockade, where we then were, there was no opportunity to spend it, and he carried the bills around in his cap for two months "fearing each bush an officer." One unhappy day the officer of the deck accosted him rather abruptly, and Trusty, taking off his cap in his bewilderment, the bills escaped and wafted hither and thither by the breeze, finally lodging in the lee scupper, followed in their flight by the curious eyes of the officer and the horrified ones of the unhappy Trusty.

Well, Trusty got thirty days, bread and water, in double irons, and three months' loss of pay, by a sentence of a summary court-martial, but he never reformed, and here he was again.

Upon his arrival at the mast I said:

"Trusty, where is this man's shirt?"

With the countenance of a dusky angel, and the honest, truthful eye of innocence, he replied as follows:

"Mr. D., I know very well that I have done many wrong things while on board this ship, that I have stolen things, and that I have been guilty of falsehood on many occasions; but now, sir, everything is different. I have become a different boy, sir, and shall never steal or do wrong any more. I've got religion, sir, me and Charley Young. We got it off of Jimmy Daggs (Jimmy was a pious contraband we picked up in the Mississippi River). We got it last week, sir, and you will never have occasion to punish me again."

Examination, nevertheless, revealed the missing shirt neatly folded in Trusty's bag, and poor Trusty was led away by the tormentors.

At eight bells (8 P. M.) the executive officer, after a personal examination, reports everything secure to the commander, the anchor watch is set, and at two bells (9 P. M.), "tattoo," then quiet reigns. At 10 P. M. the ward room lights are extinguished, unless extended by special permission, and reported out to the commander, and the day in port is ended. A day at sea, as you will see hereafter, *never* ends.

LETTER IV.

THE DAY BEGINS—THE MARINES—A LITTLE STORY—
HOW THE BOATS ARE MANNED—" ALL HANDS UP
ANCHOR "—" MAKE SAIL "—THE BOATSWAIN AND
THE ADMIRAL—" ONE OF THEM 'ERE KINGS " AND
THE WIND SAIL—THE LOG—TACKING AND WEAR-
ING SHIP.

THE DAY COMMENCES

On board ship at midnight with the midwatch; eight
bells is 12 o'clock, midnight; one bell is half-past 12;
two bells 1 o'clock; three bells half-past 1, and so on
until eight bells, 4 o'clock, commencing again at one
bell and arriving at eight bells at 8 o'clock A. M., so
that four bells, for example, may be 2, 6 or 10 o'clock
A. M. or P. M.

THE MARINES.

The larger ships have a marine guard for police
and guard duty, a sentry being stationed over the
" scuttle butt," which contains the allowance of fresh
drinking water for the men, to prevent its being
carried away or wasted; a sentry is placed over the
" brig," in charge of prisoners, one in the gangway
and one as orderly at the cabin door with a corporal
and sergeant of the guard in charge. The guard is

3

commanded by a lieutenant usually, the flagship generally having a captain as senior officer.

One day the lieutenant of marines happened to be in the cabin when the orderly came in and took off his hat; he took the first opportunity to tell him that "a soldier never uncovers" when he has his equipments on. Well, the orderly went into the cabin again, shortly after, and in accordance with his late instructions kept his hat on. The captain did not notice it at first, and went on to give him some message; but suddenly observing the hat, he stopped and asked angrily:

"What are you doing with that hat on?"

"A soldier never uncovers," replied the orderly.

"He don't, eh?" said the skipper, "I'll show you whether he does or not," and he bounced the son of Mars. I noticed after that, that the orderlies always took off their hats and bowed low when entering the presence of the irascible commander.   .

There is, of course, some feeling between the seamen and the marines, as the latter are frequently brought in collision with the former as enforcers of law, but the contempt of seamen for marines as popularly believed, is exaggerated.

A STORY.

I remember on one occasion we were sitting on the forecastle, smoking in the twilight, about 7.30 P. M., the ship running along under easy sail, when the lookout on the foreyard reported "light ho!" The master's mate in charge of the forecastle had frequently heard the officer of the deck question the lookout as to color of light, red, white, fixed, flash, revolving, etc., in order to identify the light-house to the satisfaction of the navigator, who is responsible for the position of the ship at all times; so in order to show his intelligence he asked:

"Where away?"

"Two points off the starboard bow, sir."

"Is it a white light or a *black* one?" shouted the incipient admiral.

Our laughter was turned into a convulsion by the prompt appearance of the orderly, with a message from the captain, who happened to be on the quarter deck, who, placing himself in position saluted and said:

"Mr. Smith."

"Sir."

"The captain's compliments, sir, and you are a disgrace to the ship, sir."

"Aye, aye, sir," said Smith, and the orderly faced about and returned to his post without a smile.

One day Smith went into the cabin with an application for promotion to the grade of acting master.

The cheerful old skipper looked up amiably, and said:

"Well, sir, what do *you* want?"

"If you please, sir," said Smith timidly, "*everyone* is being promoted now, sir, and I should like to be an acting master."

"Oh! you would, eh?" sneeringly returned the captain, "Why in the devil don't you apply for the position of a rear admiral, you are just about as fit for one as the other. Get out, sir," and he got.

THE BOATS.

As I have previously stated, each boat has its coxswain and regular crew, and the boat is designated as the gig—1st, 2d, 3d, and 4th cutter, barge, launch and dingey. In the S—— the boats were named, as the Daisy, Gypsy, Juanita, Zouave, Rattler, Lillie, etc., and instead of the ordinary custom of having the boatswain's mate "call away the 2d cutter," the bugler blew a call which was more musical, and attracted the attention of each of the boat's crew quicker than the other. The call for the gig or Daisy, was two bars of the soldiers' chorus, from "Faust;" the Gypsy, had the Gypsy song in "Rosedale;" the Lillie, "Lord Bateman was a Noble Lord," from the same play, while the Juanita had a tune of the same name; another tune was called "all boats," and at that signal, I have seen every boat manned, shoved off, and lying on oars in line ahead in forty seconds, without previous warning.

By the application of company drill to boats, as individuals, signals can be made from the ship, the hauling down of the same being the order for execution, and any number of boats were thus handled at will without a word.

CALLING THE BOATS AWAY.

When a boat is called away the boat keeper drops his boat to the gangway, the crew take their seats, and the coxswain reports to the officer of the deck that the boat is manned. Being told to "shove off," he gives the order in an under-tone,

"Shove off,"

"Up oars,"

"Let fall,"

"Give way."

The bow oarsmen, up oars together, let fall, and take stroke with the stroke oar without any order.

On nearing the wharf,

"In bow,"

"Way enough,"

"Toss,"

are the usual orders;

"Give way port,"

"Hold water starboard,"

"Ease starboard,"

"Ease your oars,"

and when it is wished to cease rowing, the order is simply,

"Oars,"

preceded, generally, from the coxswain with,

"Stand by to lay on your oars."

When boats are fitted with trailing lines, the order changes to,

"Out oars,"

"Trail bow," etc.;

"Give way strong,"

"Lift her,"

"Break her up, bullies," etc.,

are a few of the choice terms for encouraging a crew to pull.

"ALL HANDS UP ANCHOR"

Was the morning salutation to those who had not been included in the usual call of "all hands" at daylight the next day, and speculation was rife as to our destination. On board a man-of-war no one knows when the ship is going, or where, and you are just as likely to be off for Japan in the course of the day as not.

GETTING UNDER WEIGH.

There was a hurrying to and fro as the men repaired to their stations for getting under weigh; the captains of tops aloft to see that their running gear was clear and ready for quick work. The gunner and his gang got up and passed the heavy messenger, which, passing round the capstan and forward through the manger, passed the hawse-holes near the chain, and performing an endless circuit, drew in the chain with it, being attached thereto with nippers and devil's claws. The carpenter shipped and swiftered in the capstan bars, on spar and gun-deck, one above the other, and the order was given:

"Man the bars; heave round."

As the chain comes slowly in to the inspiriting music of the fife, the men keeping step to the music, it is cleaned, and payed below into the chain lockers, where it is tiered by the tierers. When the chain is "short" the order is given:

"MAKE SAIL."

Sail is set as previously described, and the yards braced, according to the direction you wish to cast the ship; say main yards braced up with starboard braces, and fore and mizzen with port braces. As the mizzen or crossjack (crawjick) braces lead forward the main and mizzen would be braced alike, and the fore in the opposite direction. The bars are again manned and the anchor lifted by the chain to the hawse-hole, the yards are braced, jib hoisted, spanker set, and the ship stands on under easy sail until the "cat," which is a heavy purchase from the cat-head, is hooked, and the anchor lifted to the cat-head clear of the water. The fish then hooks the arm of the anchor and pulls it upon the bill-board and the anchor is then secured for sea.

THE BOATSWAIN AND THE ADMIRAL.

One day one of our large steam frigates was getting under weigh, and the anchor came up "foul," with the chain wrapped around the "fluke." The officer of the forecastle, a lieutenant, reported "Foul anchor, sir," and proceeded to clear it. The executive officer in a few minutes went forward on the forecastle to try and hasten matters. Soon the captain nervously came on the forecastle, followed by the admiral. Two midshipmen, stationed on the main deck forward at the chains, seeing that there was rank enough on the forecastle to bring the ship by the head, also climbed up. As all of these experienced and intelligent officers were leaning over the bows, looking at a poor seaman, sitting, half submerged, on an arm of the anchor, on half a ton of mud, the old boatswain, who was astraddle of "the cat-head," yelled at the man:

"What are you putting that strap on *there* for?" Put it where I told you."

The man pointed up at the admiral, and said:

" *He* says put it here."

"*He!*" says the boatswain, "What in the devil does *he* know about it?"

The admiral danced around for a minute, and hollered "for a stick to hit that old man," but then concluded to withdraw and attend to his own business.

WITH SAILS SET.

The ship being fairly under weigh, the order was given:

"Aloft and loose the royals and topgallant sails, clear away the flying jib,"

"Man the sheets and halliards,"

"Let fall,"

"Sheet home,"

"Hoist away."

The yards were trimmed, the courses let fall, and the ship was under all plain sail. As we stretched away to the eastward, the ship was hauled on the wind, the bowlines, which steady out the leech of the sail forward, to prevent its readily catching aback, hauled out, windsails trimmed, and the decks washed and cleared for ready work.

"ONE OF THEM 'ERE KINGS" AND THE "WINDSAIL."

A "windsail" is a large canvas pipe or shoot, open on one side near the top, with wings to catch the wind and drive it down the hatch to the lower decks. These wings are spread by small ropes called **bowlines**, and, of course, must be trimmed every time there is a change of wind or course. You remember the story of one of our ships lying at Naples? On being visited by the king and his suite, one of the latter, with cocked hat, moustache, sword, etc., was exploring the ship and mistook the main hatch wind-sail for a mast, I suppose, and leaned against it. The officer of the deck was promptly advised of the accident by the boatswain's mate, who said:

"Excuse me, sir, but I think one of them 'ere kings has fell down the main hatch, sir."

"DEAD RECKONING.

As we were about to lose sight of land the navigator was sent for to take his "departure," or distance from some known headland to commence the "dead reckoning" from. The log was hove and the midshipman of the watch reported "ten six, sir."

"THE LOG."

A log chip is about the size of a fourth of a half-barrel head, a quadrant leaded on the circumference, with a hole in each corner. The log-line attaches to two corners, with an attachment to the third corner by a plug that on a smart pull comes out and allows the log chip to swim on edge, offering little resistance to the water. The log-line is marked with a white rag for strayline, and every 47.3 feet thereafter with a knot, with half knots midway. A sand glass marking twenty-eight seconds is used, and bears the same proportion to an hour that 47.3 feet does to a sea mile. The line is wound on a reel, the log chip adjusted and thrown from the weather quarter, sinking below the surface in an upright position. The strayline takes it out of the eddy of the ship and the glass is turned as the white rag passes the rail; when the sand runs out the holder cries "out," the line is checked and the line read to the nearest knot, and estimated for fathoms, as ten knots six fathoms. The ship was going ten and three-quarter knots per hour by the log.

"READY ABOUT"—TACKING SHIP.

"Ready about,"

"Stations for stays,"

"Everybody on deck to tack ship,"
was an intimation that we were bound to the southward.

As the men repaired to their stations the helm was eased down, and as the foresail began to lift, the order was given,

"Helms alee,"
at which the head sheets were eased off. As the ship came up with the wind, nearly ahead,

"Rise main tack and sheet,"
was given, so that the heavy tack and sheet blocks on

the clews of the mainsail would swing clear of the boats, and just as the pennant showed the wind dead ahead, and the spanker flapped warningly, the quick, sharp order of,

"Haul taut," "mainsail haul,"

was given, at which the after-yards were swung swiftly and braced up on the other tack.

"Head braces,"

"Haul well taut,"

and when you are sure that the ship is round on the other tack,

"Let go and haul,"

bracing round the head-yards by main strength, as being aback they have to be pulled against the wind until sharp up enough to begin to draw with the main. The S—— tacked beautifully, never losing her "way in stays." Some ships are less quick, and gather stern board after main-yards are swung, and you have to be careful to shift your helm and not get your ship "in irons," which is when she goes neither way except astern.

"WEARING A SHIP"

Is when you put your helm up and go round the other way.

You know the story of the whaler that came into New Bedford, after having been gone about three years, with only about 150 barrels of oil. One of the owners coming on board asked, in the course of the conversation, the usual courteous question:

"Well, captain, how did you like your ship?"

"Oh, pretty well," said the grumbler, "but she wouldn't 'wear nor stay.'"

"Well, I'm blessed if you didn't *stay* until you *wore* her all out," somewhat bitterly replied the unlucky proprietor.

SETTING STUDDING SAIL.

The weather continuing pleasant, and the wind hauling more aft, the captain, after church, ordered the studding sails set.

The stu'n's'ls are set on booms, which are rigged out on the topsail, lower yards, and from side of ship. projecting an additional sail as topg'll't, topm'st and lower stu'n's'ls.

"Get all your port stu'n's'ls ready for setting," is the order, then,

"Rig out, hoist away the stu'n's'ls," getting the tacks well out, then yards snug up, trimming down the sheets according to the position of the yards. The stu'n's'ls are taken in in the same manner.

"Stand by to take in all the port stu'n's'ls, lower away,"

" Haul down,"

" Rig in,"

starting the tacks when the yards are down to the booms.

LETTER V.

SHORTENING SAIL.

About seven P. M. (six bells in the second dog-watch) it began to freshen up, so that the captain directed the officer of the deck to take in the royals and flying jib. The ship was standing along to the southward, about two points free, the wind being abeam, going about eleven knots, this being her best point of sailing. The port watch of hammocks was piped down, the starboard watch having the eight hours out, and everything was made snug and clear for running.

THE LOOKOUTS.

As it was now quite dark, the masthead lookout was called down, and the regular lookouts stationed. There is a lookout at the starboard cat-head, one at the port cat-head, starboard and port gangways and starboard and port quarters. It is their duty to keep a bright lookout and to report anything that they see, promptly, to the officer of deck. At every stroke of the bell, that is, every half hour, they call their station, in the above order, to show that they are wide awake. Some of the responses are very funny, especially during the first part of a cruise, before the men have quite learned what is required of them.

One landsman called "starboard gangway" all right, and when all had finished, fearing that he had neglected some part of his duty, startled the officer of the deck with the addition,

"And *I* am here,"

provoking that somewhat impatient official to inquire:

"You?   Who in the d—l are you?"

REEFING TOPSAILS.

The wind increased during the first watch, so that the captain decided to reduce sail; accordingly the officer of the deck notified me, just before midnight, that "it was reef topsails."

I came on deck and relieved the officer of the deck in time to call the mid watch, and as "reef topsails" means "*all hands,*" the unfortunate starboard watch were obliged to stay on deck, with the port watch, and help.

"On deck *everybody* reef topsails,"

was the order, and in a few minutes the men were at their stations.   It was then blowing quite fresh; too fresh, indeed, for a landsman to go aloft.   I however took in the topgallant sails and gave the orders:

"Man the topsail clewlines and buntlines,"

"Hands by the topsail halliards,"

"Haul taut,"

"Round in the weather topsail braces,"

"Settle away the topsail halliards,"

"Clew down,"

"Haul out the reef tackles,"

"Pull up the buntlines,"

"Stand by to lay aloft and take one reef in the topsails,"

"Aloft, topmen,"

"Man the boom tricing lines,"

"Trice up,"

"Lay out and take one reef."

The men were up and out on the yard as quickly as the orders were given, and picking up the sail lighted it to windward to enable the captain of the top, at the weather earring, to haul it well out and up on the yard; then,

"Light out to leeward and tie away,"

"All ready with the main, sir,"

"All ready with the fore, sir."

The mizzen always reports first, being a smaller sail and having no booms to trice. They generally report whether ready or not, trusting to their custom of getting through first to carry them out.

"Stand by the booms,"

"Lay in,"

"Down booms,"

"Lay down from aloft,"

"Man the tops'l halliards,"

4

"Tend the braces,"

"Ease away the gear,"

"Hoist away the topsails,"

"*Stamp and go—walk away with her !*"

are the usual terms of encouragement, and the top-sail yards are hoisted and braced in a little more than before, the topgallant sails are set, and the watch goes below to be called again at 4 A. M.

An old captain ordered that if the men would reef topsails in three minutes, he would serve out an extra tot of grog—splice the main brace, as it is called. Away went the men, and the first lieutenant reported "two minutes and fifty-five seconds, sir."

"Now," said the old rascal, "I know you can do it in three minutes, and if you *don't* next time I'll put every man of you in irons."

SUNDAY ON SHIPBOARD.

The next morning the wind moderated and sail was made again, the officer of the morning watch having shaken the reefs out of the topsails, washed decks and freshened things up generally for Sunday. At 9.30 A. M. quarters and inspection, and then the bell tolled for church. Divine service is generally held Sunday morning on board a man-of-war, the men being seated on capstan bars round about the spar deck capstan, in pleasant weather, which forms a very convenient pulpit for the chaplain.

WHY THEY HURRIED TO SERVICE.

A visitor on board a man-of-war, before the stoppage of the grog ration, on witnessing the haste displayed by the men in getting to church service, said:

"Why, you don't *have* to go to church, do you, unless you *want* to?"

"Oh, no," replied the man, "we don't *have* to, only we lose our grog if we don't."

The *grog* days are over now, however, in the United States navy.

> "Now mess-mates pass the bottle round,
> It is the last, remember,
> For our grog must stop, and our spirits drop,
> On the first day of September.

> "All hands to 'splice the main brace' call,
> But we'll splice it now, in sorrow,
> For the spirit-room key will be laid away,
> Forever, on to-morrow."

THE STORY ABOUT THE COMMODORE.

They tell a story of an old commodore, at the Boston yard, who forbade the chaplain to commence service in the chapel before the arrival of his royal highness; so when the burly form of the commodore entered the chapel door, he began,

"The Lord is in His holy temple, let all the earth," etc.

The commodore would then comfortably compose himself for a nap, confident that the country was quite safe, and "that the service was not going to the d——l," at least that day.

One Sunday morning the commodore was roused from his nap by something out of the usual routine being announced from the pulpit, and he sternly addressed the chaplain with:

"What's that? What's that?"

The chaplain demurely repeated the notice that,

"By order of the bishop of this diocese, divine service will be performed in this chapel on Thursday evening next, beginning at half-past seven o'clock."

"By *whose* order?"

"By order of the bishop of this diocese, sir."

"Well," thundered the commodore, "I'll let you know that *I* am bishop of *this* diocese, and when I want service in this chapel I'll let you know. "Pipe down;" and he cleared the chapel.

On one occasion he heard a different voice in the pulpit from usual, and looking up he asked:

"Who is that up there? Is that you, Billy McMasters?"

"Yes, sir."

(Billy was a religious foreman in the yard, who sometimes helped the chaplain along.)

"Come down out of that," thundered the commodore, "when I want a relief for the chaplain I'll appoint one; don't you ever let me catch you up there again," and he cleared the *chapel again.*

Another eccentric commander, with a taste for theology, startled the chaplain one Sunday when he came up in his robes, by saying:

"I'll relieve you, sir, to-day."

He accordingly read a chapter from Genesis, and finished up at,

"And the Lord called unto Adam, and said, 'Why hast thou eaten of the fruit that I commanded ye not to eat.'"

"Now, my men, what do you think Adam said? Why, instead of coming out strong, and allowing that *he* did it, he did what the meanest landsman in the ship wouldn't have done; and what do you suppose that was? Why, he laid it on a woman."

"Pipe down," and church was over.

SUMMARY COURTS-MARTIAL.

One day I was ordered as presiding officer of a summary court-martial for the trial of another inveterate thief, also colored, like the previously alluded to Trusty. The trial was simply a matter of form, as everybody knew that he had stolen time and again, but the law prohibited the punishment of a man with any severity, except by sentence of a summary court-martial.

WHAT THE PRISONER WANTED TO KNOW.

After the testimony of several witnesses in behalf of the prosecution, all tending to criminate the prisoner, I asked him the usual question, before the withdrawal of the last one,

" Do you desire to ask the witness any questions ? "

" Yes, I do, I want to know, master-at-arms, if you kissed dat book to tell de truf, or just to tell lies on me, dats what I want to know."

The question being ruled as irrelevant, I then asked him if *he* desired to call any witnesses in his defense.

" Witnesses! Not much; you got witnesses enough now to *hang* me."

The unhappy moke consequently was sentenced to thirty days' bread and water and three months' loss of pay, at the end of which time he emerged, looking, if anything, fatter and more complacent than before.

ANCHORING IN HAMPTON ROADS.

The wind and weather continuing fair we passed between the capes of the Chesapeake and anchored in Hampton Roads on the following afternoon, where we found a large number of men-of-war, also at anchor, awaiting orders from the admiral.

SENIOR OFFICER.

It is a good deal of a nuisance to be in the presence of a "Senior Officer." You have to follow his motions entirely, strike the bell at the same time, loose sail and cross yards by signal; the men must be dressed in white or blue, as are those of the flag-ship; and it is more than probable that the admiral will signal suddenly, just when you don't want it, to "arm and equip boats," passing in review under the stern of the flag-ship for inspection to see if each boat be armed with so many rifles, cutlasses and revolvers, and supplied with cook stove, fish lines, lead patches for covering shot holes, spare oars, hammers, nails, etc., with fresh water in breakers for drinking, pork, hardtack, flints and steel (for matches are forbidden on board ship), with which the boat is laden nearly to the gunwale.

The admiral detailed us temporarily for guardship, which required us to inspect every vessel, passing in and out, to see if papers were in order, and vessel properly cleared.

HOW THE COMMANDER-IN-CHIEF OF THE ARMY WAS "BROUGHT TO."

One day the officer of the deck hastily called to me that he had hailed a steamer twice with no response. I sprang upon the bridge and hailed the steamer with,

"Stop your engine, sir."

As he did not stop I sung out:

"Pivot guns crew to your quarters."

The men came aft with a jump, and down came the temporary bulwarks, around swung the gun, and "*bang*" went a hundred pound shell about as many yards to the right of the steamer.

Well, she turned round so quick that it seemed as if she might capsize. The captain came jumping out of the cabin to know what was the matter, and ruefully exclaimed that I had broken all the glass in the cabin windows.

I called a midshipman and sent him on board the steamer with orders to put on airs, and "want to know, you know," etc.

He soon returned, having permitted the steamer to proceed, reporting:

"Well, sir, I went aboard and sternly asked the captain for his papers. He pointed to an army officer standing near, saying:

"'There are my papers.'

"I didn't understand, and he added:

" 'Major-General Halleck, sir, commanding the armies of the United States.'

" 'You can proceed,' said I, and returned aboard."

LETTER VI.

HEAVING THE LEAD.

The depth of water is ascertained on board ship by "heaving the lead." An ordinary hand lead line is from fifteen to twenty fathoms in length and is marked at one, two, three, five and seven fathoms, with strips of leather, colored rags, and at ten with "a piece of round hole with a leather in it," as I heard a small boy once say.

The lead weighs five, seven or ten pounds, according to the depth of water and the speed of the ship. The thrower generally stands in the "chains" outside the rail of the ship, with a canvas strap around his waist to prevent his falling overboard, and swings the lead, launching it well forward, feels the bottom as the line comes up and down, and chants, "by the mark five," or "by the deep six," as the case may be.

An Irishman, who could do everything, was sent into the chains one day to heave the lead. He commenced chanting away at intervals until the officer of the deck, despairing of making out the depth of water, came up and asked him what he said.

"Divil a word did I say, sur. I learned the tune only and never caught the words," replied Dennis.

At sea, when the water is deeper, the deep sea (pro-
nounced dipsey) lead is used.

A Dutchman at the lead line, who had not exactly
caught the words, chanted in a Dutch monotone:

"Blainty of va-a-ter he-ere. Not quite zo mooch
va-a-ter he-ere. You'd petter keep avay from here,"
and as the ship struck in three fathoms of water,

"Didn't I to-old you so-o?"

THE SKIPPER WHO KNEW BY THE TASTE.

You remember the poem reciting the gift possessed
by the skipper of a Nantucket schooner, of being
able, by the taste, to tell exactly where the schooner
was. An incredulous mate, on one occasion, rubbed
the well tallowed lead in the earth of a box of plants,
which some lover of flowers had brought from Nantucket, and carried it in to the slumbering captain,
as a specimen of the sounding just taken. The skipper rubbed his eyes and sleepily tasted. Springing
from his bunk, he rushed on deck exclaiming:

"Nantucket's sunk, and here we are right over old
Marm Hackett's garden!"

SALUTES AND CEREMONIES.

While we lay in Hampton Roads we were constantly visiting and receiving visits from other officers of the squadron, as well as from some French
and English officers, whose ships were lying, tempo-

rarily, in the Roads, and the side was being piped, and two, four, six or eight side boys constantly rushing to the gangway, as officers of different rank came on board.

When the President of the United States visits one of our men-of-war, he is received at the gangway by the admiral, commanding officer, and all the officers of the ship, in full uniform, the crew at quarters for inspection, the marine guard drawn up with the band on the quarter deck, the national flag is displayed at the main, the drummer gives four ruffles, the band plays the national air, and a salute of twenty-one guns is fired; the same ceremony also taking place on his leaving; the yards may also be manned unless forbidden. On one occasion when the President visited one of our ships informally, dispensing with salute and ceremony, one of the men rather indignantly asked another, "who that lubber was on the quarter deck that didn't 'douse his peak' to the commodore?"

"Choke your luff, will you," was the reply, "that's the President of the United States."

"Well! ain't he got manners enough to salute the quarter deck if he is?"

"*Manners!* What does he know about *manners?* I don't suppose he was ever out of sight of land in his life."

On one occasion while lying in a foreign port, an officer from shore, I have forgotton of what rank, came on board officially to visit the ship. I interviewed his aid to know what the Dago's rank was. (Sailors call everybody that speaks Spanish, Italian and Portuguese, Dagos.) He replied that he was entitled to six guns. I said we give five or seven guns, but never six, take seven; but no, he persisted six guns was enough, and so we fired him his salute of six guns.

The Chinese national salute is only three guns, and saves a great deal of expense in the way of powder.

BOY OVERBOARD.

We had a number of apprentices on board the S——, and they were drilling one afternoon at the various drills, and among others there was a crew in the fore chains exercising "heaving the lead." It seems that, contrary to express orders, one of the boys was standing on one of the upper half ports which close the gundeck port-holes. When open these ports are triced up on their hinges and kept level by the port lanyard. Another boy also jumped on to the port, and their united weight broke the lanyard; the port falling, threw one of the boys into the water. I happened to be standing on the gundeck, near the ward room hatch, and hearing the unusual rush on deck, sprang to the hatchway.

"Boy overboard, sir."

I ran aft to the life buoy, which hangs on the quarter, and pulled the bell-pull, dropping the buoy instantly. I could see nothing of the boy, however, although I judged that the rapid current of the Delaware River would have carried him down to about where the life buoy was then floating. The boat keeper in the gig, which was lying at the lower studding-sail boom, quickly dropped his boat astern. Two boats, which were exercising at oars close by, pulled promptly up, but in vain, the little fellow did not come up.

I turned, and looked forward at the eager sea of faces turned to me, as if to read in my countenance the fate of the boy.

"Go on with your exercises," I said shortly.

And almost instantly one could hear "by the ma-a-rk five" from the very spot from which the boy fell.

"Present arms,"

"Run in,"

"Serve vent and sponge,"

from the other sections drilling close by, and for the time the little drowned shipmate was forgotten.

A few days afterward, when the body was found, an ugly mark on the forehead showed that he had probably been stunned by striking his head against the gun in falling, and did not therefore come up.

We had a sad sort of a funeral, for the little fellow was a great favorite with all. A few days after a woman in deep black came on board "to see the captain." The captain, who was really a great big tender-hearted fellow, though he would scorn to acknowledge such a thing, suspected that it was the boy's mother, and gently suggesting that it was the first lieutenant that she wished to see, "slid out" quietly, and sent me in to "tell her all about it."

"You officers don't have much of anything to do on board of ship except in time of war, do you?"

I have often wished that I could capture a few of the idiots that talk in that way, and set them at work—real *work* on board ship for about a month. I think that they would begin to realize that they had been only *playing* hitherto.

I had to listen to this poor woman's story, and see her tears and sobs as she explained:

"You know, sir, that poor little Dick was a son of my first husband, sir, and then, sir, you know times was hard, and I didn't know what to do, and Mr. L——, sir, came along and I thought it would be best, you know, sir, and make a home for Dick, and I married again. Well, Dick didn't seem to get along well with his father, and he was forever at me about him, so I shipped him as an apprentice boy, as you know, sir, and now the poor little fellow's dead, and he *might* have lived, you know, sir."

I wonder if any one thinks that it was *easy* for me to listen to this sad story; *easy* for me to try to console this poor mother in her great grief; and *easy* for me to go back on deck and run the vast, never-ceasing machine of a man-of-war with my heart still like a great lump in my throat.

LETTER VII.

BOXING THE COMPASS.

"Can you box the compass, sir?"

"Well, sir, that depends upon the size and shape of your compass!" was the reply of an embryo mid-shipman one day on board ship.

That is all very well as a story, but no person can be on board a ship more than a week, without finding out that he must learn the compass if he would understand much of what is going on around him.

The four cardinal points of the compass are north, south, east and west, from the initials of which the word "news" is formed and derived, being collected from all directions. As it is necessary to steer between these points, subdivisions had to be made; as, half-way between north and east became northeast, and the opposite point southwest; half way between north and northeast became north northeast, and between east and northeast, of course, east northeast; this, not being minute enough, was subdivided again, and became north by east, and east by north, etc., the learner remembering that there are thirty-two points of eleven and a quarter degrees each; that the initials of any point exchange exactly with the oppo-

5

site point, as, the opposite of northeast by north, is, of course, south west by south.

Boxing the compass consists in repeating the names of the points, commencing at any point, and going either way round to the place of beginning; as, nor', nor' by east, nor' nor'east, nothe-east by nor', nothe-east; nothe-east by east, east nothe-east, east by nor', east; east by sou', east southeast, south east by east, southeast; southeast by south, south southeast, south by east, south; south by west, south southwest, southwest by south, southwest, southwest by west, west southwest, west by south, west; and so on.

You remember the sailor, who didn't know the Lord's Prayer, upon hearing the chaplain repeat it, asked him to say it backwards and triumphantly proved the better knowledge of his profession by boxing the compass backwards and forwards.

" How do you head?" called the captain one day to the man at the wheel.

" Nor'west by west, a half west, westerly, sir," was the answer.

" Put another west to that, and I'll give you a tot of grog," said the skipper.

" Aye, aye, sir," said the quick-witted helmsman. " Nor'west by west, a half west, westerly, Captain West."

Fortunately for the story and the helmsman, the skipper's name *was* West.

VARIATION OF THE COMPASS.

Variation of the compass is the difference between the *true* north and the north as shown by the compass, and varies with the position or location of the observer; the variation of the compass is marked on the charts as ascertained by observation, and should be corrected from time to time, as it is not constant, but varies from year to year. Variation is designated, easterly or westerly, according as the true north is to the eastward or westward of that point as shown by the compass. The Navy Department requires that observations, which are called azimuths, or amplitudes, be taken daily, to find the variation of the compass, and that a record of the same be kept; from an average of these observations the charts are kept corrected.

DEVIATION OF THE COMPASS.

There is another correction to be applied to a compass, which is called deviation; this is a local error in the ship itself, and must be ascertained, and either removed or corrected.

In an iron ship, like the ill-fated Huron, surrounded as the compass was with iron guns and iron bolts, you will readily see that this sensitive magnet, the compass needle, would be attracted or repelled variously, according to the direction of the ship's head; the compass being aft, the greater bulk of iron, attractive or repellant, according to which pole of the needle was nearest, would naturally be forward; if the ship was headed north, the deviation would probably be at a minimum; if east or west, at a maximum.

HOW TO CORRECT THIS DEVIATION.

In order to ascertain the deviation, the ship is swung from a buoy, with her head successively on each point of the compass, a bearing is taken of another observer stationed at a considerable distance on shore, who at the same instant notes the bearing of the ship, and telegraphs the reading of his compass, which has no deviation; if the two bearings are the reverse of each other, there is no deviation on that point; if they differ, the difference is the deviation, and so on for each point of the compass.

The deviation may be easterly, the variation westerly, and the difference would be the correction when applied to the compass, when heading, say northwest; but when heading southeast the deviation would more likely be westerly and would be added to the variation as a correction.

Generally, where the deviation is great and varied, it is corrected by two magnets laid in the deck, in such positions, determined by experiment, as will overcome and correct the attraction of the ship.

I remember on one occasion the ship ran away, and like to have got overboard, because some careless chap stowed his *knife* away in the binnacle.

HOW BOATS ARE LOWERED IN A SEAWAY.

There is great difficulty in manning a boat at sea in rough weather. The boat rises and falls with each wave, while the ship rolls violently from side to side, making it no easy matter to avoid either swamping the boat or dashing it in pieces against the side of the ship. The only chance in the boat's favor is in the practicability of dropping it suddenly into the water from the davits, allowing it to shove off instantly from the side of the ship. No one can appreciate the extreme danger of lowering a boat in heavy weather unless he has witnessed the operation itself.

I have seen a boat being hoisted to the davits; one man in the bow at the forward fall, another aft to hook the after fall; the boat plunging up and down, the ship rolling fearfully, as only gunboats *can* roll; the falls snatched and manned ready to "run away with her" at the order. The officer of the deck watches for a smooth time to "hook on," then "run

her up." If successful the boat rises above the rail
before the ship has time to roll again; if not, the
boat flies out from the side almost at right angles
with the davits, and crash! comes back against the
ship's side. In lowering a boat the bow and stern
men at the stoppers have to look alive and unhook
the falls together, or the after one a little the first,
as should the after fall hold, the boat will inevitably
swing round and fill as the ship goes ahead, and then
good-bye boat.

A LOWERING APPARATUS.

In order to launch a boat surely and successfully a
boat lowering apparatus is used in the navy, which I
here briefly describe. After the boat is hoisted the
ordinary fall is unhooked and the boat suspended by
chains, the link of chain in the bow and stern passing
over a tumbler or hinge, the chain coming then to
a small barrel or capstan inboard. When the boat is
to be lowered the crew takes its place and the boat is
lowered by the chain until within a few feet of the
water, when by pulling a small chain, which runs
round the inside of the gunwale, the tumblers are
released, the hinges fly up, allowing the links of chain
to slip off, and the boat is free, bow and stern at the
same instant. There are several patents, all based on
the principle described, for lowering boats in a seaway.

Usually boat-falls hook to a ring and link in the bow and stern of the boat, and it is difficult for the men to hook on simultaneously. This is somewhat obviated in the "whale" boats, a term generally applied to boats sharp at both ends, by having rings instead of hooks in the lower blocks which hook on to the outside stem and stern of boats with a snap like a dog chain, to keep them from unhooking. When a boat is being lowered in heavy weather, the the sea or long painter in the bow of the boat is always led out and forward, and made fast in the gangway to prevent accidents.

WHO LET GO THAT FOR'UD FALL?

There is an amusing sketch in a book of etchings by Park Benjamin, Jr., a midshipman in the navy, of a boat hanging by the stern fall to the davit, the bow nearly in the water, two or three midshipmen in various ridiculous attitudes falling into the water, with another striking out for a swim, the whole easily explained by the interrogation,

"Who let go that for'ud fall?"

AS RELATED BY THE MIDSHIPMAN.

Speaking of boats reminds me of a conversation which took place in a boat belonging to a German frigate on one occasion. The midshipman, who had charge of the boat had been visiting one of our ships and was much pleased with the position, privilege and duties of our midshipmen on board, which seemed more favorable than in his own service. On returning, however, to the landing on shore accompanied by a couple of our midshipmen, it occurred to him to ask:

"Wat atority do you haf in de poats?"

"Which?" said the Yankee.

"Vell, I mean of de mens don't do yoost as you say vat you do mit 'em?"

"Oh!" replied one, "I report them to the first lieutenant, when I return to the ship, and have them punished."

"Ish dat all?" said the German, "I shows you mein atority," and he accordingly rose, and with the convenient tiller, knocked over the unoffending, stroke oarsman; and with the remark,

"Dat ish mein atority,"

he resumed his seat, perfectly satisfied that when it came to questions of real *business his* service was by far the more satisfactory.

FIRE QUARTERS.

"Ding dong," "ding dong," went the ship's bell rapidly, and from the instant rush from every part of the vessel one would have supposed that "the ship had fallen overboard."

"Fire!"

Fire is a terrible thing on shore, even when viewed from a place of safety, but transfer the scene to a ship, with the realizing sense that you have five miles of water under you, unless you put it out (I mean the fire), and you can probably understand the *deep* interest we have in fires on board ship. In order to have a fire drill effective, the fact that it is a drill, and not a real fire, must be found out afterward. The commanding officer, generally when he feels dyspeptic, I think, and hates mankind, comes browsing along, and capturing a small messenger boy sends him forward quietly to ring the ship's bell like blazes—and he *does.* I think I never have seen more perfect contentment on the face of a boy than when charged with this fiendish errand; and he rings and *rings,* until throttled by some forecastle man, who, fully appreciating his enthusiasm, having been there himself, persuades him that he was only told to ring a few taps.

At the signal every one goes to his quarters; then the first lieutenant calls out:

"Fire in the fore hold."

Down come the windsails, on go the hatch gratings and tarpaulins; every one in the masters' division, like the veterans in the late unpleasantness, seems anxious to "avoid the draft."

Away aft goes the gunner to the cabin door to get the keys of the magazines to flood them, if ordered. No. 1 gun's crew will work *this* chain pump, No. 2 *this* one in the main chains; this division of firemen form a line of buckets from starboard gangway, that one from port gangway, one from starboard quarter, another from port quarter, and so on.

Along come rushing pipemen with two lines of hose ready to flood anything and everybody, and in less than one minute a dozen lines of buckets and two lines of pipes await the order to,

"Start the water."

All this time no one knows, except the dyspeptic individual previously referred to, and the messenger, perhaps, whether there is a fire or not.

The executive officer gets even with the captain sometimes, however, if he has not been consulted, by suddenly discovering a fire aft, and,

"Fire in the cabin,"

sends a delighted stream of buckets and lines of dampish hose into the cabin, to no small inconvenience of the practical joker who started the row.

It is the duty of the commanding officer of the marine guard to post sentries over the boats to prevent their being lowered without orders from the proper authority, to release prisoners, and to hold the balance of his guard on the quarter-deck, armed and equipped, for use where needed to preserve order and discipline.

If at sea, or under way, the course of the ship is altered to bring the fire to leeward as much as possible, the reason of which is obvious.

LETTER VIII.

Shortly after our arrival at Ship Island, Gulf of
Mexico, we were ordered by the flag officer, D. G.
Farragut, to blockade the mouth of the Rio Grande
River. So, one morning bright and early the pipes of
the boatswain's mates were heard, followed by the
repeated cry of,

"All hands,"

"All hands,"

"Up all hammocks,"

"Now tumble up there,"

"Show a leg,"

"Get out of there, you idlers,"

"Clear the berth-deck, master-at-arms,"

"No one excused,"

"It's up anchor this morning."

In ten minutes the hammocks were all up and

stowed in the nettings, and the captains of the different parts of the ship were quickly moving to and fro, quietly directing their men so as to get as ready as they dared before the order "up anchor" was actually given.

In a few moments after the anchor was hove short, and in obedience to the order of the executive officer.

"Aloft, sail-loosers."

the men swarmed aloft, and in less time than it takes to write it the gallant little "Portsmouth" was under way with all plain sail, standing to the southward and westward, bound for "La Boca del Rio del Norte," as the mouth of the Rio Grande is called by our Mexican friends on the south side.

THE FIRST PRIZE.

We sailed along pleasantly without incident until almost within sight of the coast, when we discovered a schooner standing to the southward, which we quickly overhauled. Running up the French flag we were much pleased to be answered by the display of the rebel stars and bars. Amid considerable excitement a boat was lowered, and with twelve men armed to the teeth I pulled off for the schooner, the "Portsmouth" at the same time hauling down the French flag and displaying the stars and stripes at the peak. We pulled alongside, and clambering up the side of the schooner (I with my sword in my teeth, being armed to the teeth), we sprang on board, prepared to cut down almost anything—excepting, of course (I cannot tell a lie), any cherry trees. There was one poor devil on deck who was quietly steering the schooner. After lowering the sails I boldly, yet cautiously, advanced upon this man and sternly asked,

"Where is the captain, sir?"

"Oh! we're all captains here," he answered *nonchalently*, "but Captain B—— is below," he added, "if you want *him*."

We persuaded the captain and all hands to come on deck, and found that our prize was the schooner "Wave," from New Orleans, bound to the Rio Grande. We transferred his cargo of sugar to one of the supply steamers shortly afterward, and used the schooner itself as a target for exercise at great guns.

I think I got some $43 prize money about twelve years afterward from the sale of the "Wave's" cargo.

The next day we anchored off

THE MOUTH OF THE RIO GRANDE,

where some seventy merchant vessels lay at anchor. I was surprised to find that the mouth of the river appeared to be only a couple of hundreds of yards in width instead of a mile, as I had always imagined.

I found that the commander shared my opinion, and decidedly refused to believe me, as navigator of the ship, declining to accept any such dirty little river as the great river of the north. In vain I pleaded that the sun could not lie, that figures were figures. He declined to accept the situation, until I returned from boarding most of the vessels at anchor and reported that they were all under the same impression.

SAILING OVER THE ANDES.

I could not blame him. He knew the story of a young officer who was attached to a ship bound for Rio. as navigator. The captain distrusted his ability and secured all the charts of the ship so the navigator could not see them, requiring him to send in the latitude and longitude every day as usual, ascertained by observations of the sun. On the arrival of the ship in Rio the captain showed the young mathematician that by his reckoning, as sent in from day to day, the ship had skirted the Andes Mountains all the way down, being impartially sometimes on one side and sometimes on the other of the lofty range. congratulating him on the feat of balancing this sloop-of-war successfully on a mountain peak, 23,000 feet in height, without knowing it.

Of course, the navigator not having access to the

charts, could not see where his latitude and longitude
would place the ship, and supposed all the time that
he was the equal, if not the superior of Mr. C. Col-
umbus, as a navigator of the seas.   Well,

THE CAPTAIN NEVER LET UP

on me; he would not believe that that little stream
was the Rio Grande River.   I took sights every day
and required the midshipmen to take sights with me,
showing, accurately, our position by the sun; he
would not believe it, and, had it not been that an
American, who had lived in Matamoras for ten years,
and came armed with a permit from Hon. W. H.
Seward, Secretary of State, to trade, assured him on
his word of honor, that the opening in question, *was*
the Rio Grande, he never would have believed it, and
the baleful stigma of deception, want of accuracy,
and general untrustworthiness, would have been
equally shared between the sun of our solar system
and the son of my father.

The really good old gentleman has, however, long
since passed away, and I hope that he reached the
port for which he was bound, his course being
marked out for him by a skillful and unerring navigator in whom he could have implicit trust.

I had a great deal of amusement in

BOARDING THE DIFFERENT VESSELS

lying at anchor off the port. The Engiishmen would hospitably offer a " drop a sherry," proffering a brimming tumbler to carry out the idea; the Frenchmen showed their friendly feeling in cognac, and the German kindness overflowed in the shape of Schiedam schnapps, and Holland gin. One old German had a little old galiot, that looked as if it had served as a tender to old Von Tromp, when he carried the broom at his masthead in the English Channel; he had his wife, nurse and four children on board, cooped up in the little cabin, 10x12 feet, and they all seemed as fat and contented as if they occupied a *Schloss Unter den Linden*, Berlin. He was very hospitable, and was profuse in his offers of " yust a ledle more cherry cordial."

The appearance of a little German-American, shortly after, showed that the climate of Mexico—Texas, tempered by the cool breeze of the Gulf of Mexico, must have assimilated greatly with that of their own Fatherland.

We remained on the coast of Texas some two or three months, part of the time at anchor, and part of the time cruising off and on. Now and then the monotony would be varied by a terrible gale of wind called a " Norther," which put our ground-tackle or

6

our canvas to a severe test, according as we were at anchor or under sail.

THE OTHER PRIZE.

One noon we saw a sloop standing in shore toward the mouth of the river. I started in pursuit with a twelve-oared cutter, and we had a neck and neck pull to cut him off before getting within range of the guns at the mouth of river. Fortunately for us there was not much wind, and we captured the sloop within a mile and a half of her destination. It proved to be from New Orleans, with a cargo for Matamoras. So, we transferred the cargo to our own ship, and sunk the sloop.

I believe I got some $25 prize money from the capture some ten years after.

Being short of fresh water, the commander resolved to go to the mouth of the Mississippi for a supply, and we accordingly got under weigh, and after a a pleasant trip of a few days we anchored off Southwest Pass in time to participate in the capture of Forts Jackson and St. Philip.

Apropos of Mexico,

THEY TELL A STORY

of the captain of a brig at Vera Cruz who took a sailor who spoke Spanish, on shore with him to interpret for him. The conversation was somewhat as follows:

Sailor—"*Habla usted Español Señor?*"

"*Si, Señor, perfectamente bien,*" replied the Mexican.

"*Bueno,*" said the sailor, "*in cuantas dias* can you make a new main yard for the brig?"

"*No entiendo*" (I don't understand), said the Mexican.

"*No en ten day?*" said the sailor.

"Oh, come on, captain, he says he can't do it in ten days."

Another linguist on shore, at the same port, came up excitedly to a native and asked:

"Look here, Señor, ha visto usted a caballero a cavorting down the streets on a derned big gray horse with a Mexican saddle on?"

"*No entiendo?*" said the native with a peculiar shrug of his shoulders pertaining to the race.

"*No entiendo?*" don't you understand your own lingo, you infernal Dago?

The boatswain of the U. S. Portsmouth was very profane, and showed a great deal of disgust at the agricultural aspect of many of the crew, really good men, but quite unused to a man-of-war. One day he apostrophized them on the foreyard somewhat as follows:

"Pick up that sail, will you?"

"No! pass in the leech first; that's no way to stow that bunt, Oh! you farmers!"

"Hold on with that bunt jig, will you?"

"Who in the d——l told you to pull up that bunt jig? My grandmother would make a better sailor than you."

"Look aloft; the devil would have been a sailor only he couldn't look aloft," etc.

One day hearing me hail the lookout aloft,

"Fore topmast crosstrees there,"
several times without reply, the boatswain who was standing on the forecastle said:

"That's a farmer up there, sir; he don't know that he's on the crosstrees, say *haymow* and he'll jump overboard."

LETTER IX.

THE MISSISSIPPI FLEET AT THE CAPTURE OF NEW ORLEANS.

About two weeks before the passage of Forts Jackson and St. Philip by the squadron under the command of the flag officer, David G. Farragut, I was attached to the United States sloop-of-war P——; we had come to the mouth of the Mississippi for water, and Farragut directed that we should remain and join in the attack on the forts.

At this time, April, 1862, the fleet, of some twenty odd sail including the Hartford (flagship), the Brooklyn, Iroquois, Westfield and others, were anchored below the point where the river made a sharp turn before reaching the forts, while Porter's mortar flotilla, some twenty or more schooners, lay along behind the point, close in shore. The mortar schooners had clothed the tops of their low masts with branches of trees, so that they could scarcely be distinguished, as they lay behind the thick trees lining the river bank. Our commander, accordingly, ordered our spars to be dressed in the same way, and we loomed up like a line of battle ship, securing us the honor of a visit from the flag officer, with a sharp order to,

"Take those things down,"
much to the satisfaction of the executive officer and
the chagrin of the captain.

FIRE RAFTS

While thus lying at anchor, a favorite device of
the Confederates was to send down enormous fire
rafts, by which they hoped to fire some of the ships
anchored in the stream. As the current ran, at that
high condition of the water, at nearly five knots an
hour, the arrival of these rafts excited a lively interest, I can assure you.

"Send boats to tow fire rafts,"
would be the signal, nearly every night from the flagship, and away would go four of our boats toward
the approaching raft coming down the river. Two
of the large launches from the heavier classed vessels
would throw grapnels into the rafts, and the other
boats forming two lines ahead, sometimes thirty in a
line, would tow the raft slowly, but surely, across the
river, allowing it to ground and burn itself harmlessly out.

One night a monster raft, filled with turpentine,
tar and rosin, came down the river and created considerable alarm. The boats promptly tackled it, as
usual, but found that they could not stem the current,
as the raft was unusually large and difficult to handle.

About six hundred yards from us, lay, at anchor, a store ship filled with powder, shell and ammunition for the squadron; she was directly in the line of the approaching and rapidly descending fire raft; the boats made superhuman efforts to tow it across the river and swing the raft clear, but it was evident that they would be unsuccessful, when suddenly the West-field, formerly one of the New York ferryboats, seeing the danger that threatened the whole squadron, promptly slipped her chain, steamed boldly up, and, with two streams of water playing over her bow, and her crew at "fire quarters," put her nose fairly against the raft and drove it square across the river, where it grounded safely and burned out.

"*Cheers!*"

You could have heard that cheer, from nearly 7,000 throats, ten miles.

ONE OF THE MORTAR SCHOONERS

lay about 100 yards ahead of us, and a continuous line of them lay farther on up stream. Every five or ten minutes throughout the night, *bang!* went a thirteen-inch shell, up, up; its course marked, like a meteor, by the burning fuse; then, turning down, down, swiftly plunging into Fort Jackson. By carefully weighing the powder, and noting the angle of inclination during the day, they were enabled, at night, by means of range lights in the trees, to keep up an accurate fire, continuous night and day, raining those terrible shells constantly into the devoted fort; and, as by their explosion, they tore great chasms in the ground and casemates, it must have been terrible, indeed, for the defenders, who were powerless to reply.

One night a great conflagration illumined the fort, and we learned afterward that it was caused by the burning of the citadel, fired by the explosion of a shell from the mortar fleet. As it happened, the fire was so near the magazine that it could not have been opened, and had we gone by that night, we would have suffered but little from the guns of Fort Jackson and saved many valuable lives.

RUNNING THE FORTS.

On the night of the 24th of April, 1862, the signal—two red lights at the peak of the flagship—to move was observed, and the vessels got under weigh, and steamed slowly up the river. The chain, which the rebels had stretched across the river, and which had been the occasion of many an exciting and daring attempt, had been finally cut, and nothing remained but to go by the forts. It seemed almost like a plunge into the hereafter, for the "rebs," too, had gunboats above the forts, and terrible rams, ironclads, torpedoes, and what else we knew not, and to *get by* the forts didn't seem so very desirable a thing to do after all; however, there was the order, and there was no help for it. Our ship being a sailing sloop-of-war, was lashed alongside a steamer to be towed up opposite Fort Jackson and anchored, to divert the attention of that fort as much as possible from the steamers. There is such a thing as being *too* conspicuous, in having *too* much attention, and I would have preferred to have been one of those "born to blush unseen," and waste my—what do you call it?—somewhere else. Well, history tells

HOW THE GALLANT FLEET WENT BY,

amid a terrible cannonade from both forts, the easterly column of battle passing within 300 yards of the guns of St. Philip, 150 of them grinning defiance, almost on a level with the river bank; history tells how the mortar fleet rained thirteen-inch shells into the forts (I counted thirteen in the air at once); history tells how the Varuna, running fast and ahead of everybody, engaged the Governor Morgan broadside and broadside, and almost alongside, until suddenly a little ram scooted under the stern of the Morgan and rammed the Varuna so she sunk at once, her officers and crew crowding on to the forecastle, which was just out of water, alternately swearing at, and dodging the shots from the passing "rebs" flying up the river to escape the triumphant ascending fleet. History tells how the gallant old Mississippi, a side-wheel wooden frigate, which didn't know anything about rams, chased the dreaded ram, Manassas, until she ran ashore and was fired by her crew. Somebody tells how

THE FIRST LIEUTENANT OF THE BROOKLYN

(she was fighting her starboard battery and there wasn't a soul on the port side), happening to look to port, saw the Manassas approaching and about to ram the ship, recognized an old shipmate and a former officer of the Brooklyn itself, in command of her, and shouted:

"Warley, you d——d scoundrel, don't you run into us!"

and giving the Brooklyn a rank sheer to starboard avoided the full force of the blow, and not being able to do anything else, danced up and down on the bridge and fired his revolver at the ironclad; history tells how the U. S. S. P—— participated in the gallant attack, etc., but history is painfully silent as to *me*, as to *my* heroism, my-a-undaunted courage as I led my men-a-a-below the water-line. *Now*, after waiting fifteen years, I am permitted to tell the story myself—in *print*, too, and not at ten cents a line, either.

FIGHTING FORT JACKSON.

Well, we steamed up until our guns would bear on Fort Jackson and anchored, and our escort left us to the mercy of the rebel guns. A line was sent on shore from aft, and our broadside was brought to bear by springing the ship. As soon as I had seen the anchor chains secure, as that was in my department, being navigator of the ship, I repaired to the topgallant forecastle where my division was working an eight-inch shell, and a thirty-pound rifle gun. Being short of men, I acted as captain of the rifle gun, and sighted and fired the gun myself. The daylight was just breaking behind us, and we were as pretty a target as one ever saw. I could see the flash of the rebel guns, and hear the whistle of the shot, as it approached nearer and nearer, until it either struck short, or passing over screamed:

"Whar is he? whar is he?"

and plunged into the water beyond us. I trained, sighted and fired away with my rifle gun, however, taking a good long while to sight, while crouched somewhat behind it, apparently only safer than when standing up.

Just then the eight-inch gun, on being fired, jammed the carriage of the rifle gun so that I could no longer train it; in vain we tried to get the eight-inch out of the way—we could not budge it; shot and

shell were striking and exploding all around us; one
or two gunboats that failed to get by had returned
and passed down astern of us; the fleet had got by
and our mission was over; but the fort had its mission too, there being no one else in sight—all of its
guns that would bear, were trained on us—us, who
only asked to be let severely alone.

ONE LONG SHELL

(I learned afterward that it was really only seven and
a quarter inches in diameter and thirty inches in
length, but it looked as long then as the stock of the
bower anchor and as big around as a barrel) struck
short about twenty feet from us, and fortunately for
us, on the side of a wave, and rose, passing high over
the ship.   When it struck the wave first I saw it as
plain as if it were floating on the water, and half
closed my eyes, certain that it would ricochet and hit
me right in the stomach.   I drew a long breath when
it passed over, and that is what I could not have done
if it had followed the course I had marked out for it.

"Whew! bang!"

came a sixty-four pound shot over from aft.   The
captain, first lieutenant, paymaster and clerk, humbly
saluting it as it p. p. c'd over the poop and struck one
of my gun's crew, just five feet ten inches below
where I stood, bounded up, and expending itself

under the topgallant forecastle, about ten inches from my feet, rolled harmlessly down in the water ways. Well, we slipped and got out of there soon, *very* soon. The rapid current of the Mississippi never seemed so much overrated as it did to us, when we depended entirely upon it to take us out of reach of the shot and shell which the fort so carelessly flung after us.

The poor fellow who was struck was quickly carried to the main hatch and lowered, on a litter ready for the purpose, to the main hold, where the surgeons were ready in attendance, the blood pouring from his leg in great splashes, which, crimson as it was, blanched the faces of many who stood at their guns wondering if they would be next.

The doctors took off his leg, but the shock was too great, and it was my painful duty, the following day, to read the service over his now forgotten grave on a small island in the Mississippi River.

AND WE ALL WERE DODGING.

When the shot and shell were flying the thickest, an old captain of the forecastle, who was in command of the eight-inch gun, was dancing and ducking around, and I yelled at him angrily (I was even a trifle more frightened than he),

"What in the deuce are you doing, you can't dodge 'em."

"Oh, yes, you can," said he, "I did at Peiho."

It seems that the old fellow had never been under fire before, excepting when some of our ships joined the English in an attack on two forts in China, and he dated everything from the attack on the Peiho forts.

I could not help laughing, frightened as I was, as I stood on the topg'll't forecastle, and looked aft. *Whiz,* would come a shell close over the poop, and *down* would duck all hands. It was no evidence of courage at all, for one ducked involuntarily the same as one winks when the eye is threatened; but Pay, you ought to have seen Pay. He had been flattered by being made signal officer, though there were no signals to make, and was stationed on the poop. When I saw him he was holding on to the mizzen rigging and his feet, in a spasm of ducking, having slipped off the ladder, he was dangling about eight feet above the quarter deck, and holding on so tight to the mizzen rigging as to squeeze the tar out of it.

"I suppose Mr. D——," said a young lady once to me, "that you get so thoroughly accustomed to danger and being under fire that you don't mind it at all."

"On the contrary," I replied, "I never have been in serious danger more than seven or eight times since I have been in the service, and I assure you, that I was more frightened the last time, than the first."

"Why," resumed she, "a friend of mine, a Mr. Smith, he was a master's mate, I think, in the Mississippi squadron, told me that he really enjoyed it, and wasn't one bit afraid."

FARRAGUT'S JOKE ON BUTLER.

I must tell you of a joke on Gen. Benjamin F. Butler, perpetrated by Admiral Farragut. As Farragut was, strictly speaking, not much of a joker, it is but fair that he should be given credit for *this* one.

The Tennessee came dashing up the river to New Orleans, one day, and anchored near the flagship; the captain being on shore in the afternoon, was met by an officer who stated that Gen. Butler would be pleased to see him.

He accordingly waited on the general, who sternly took him to task for passing the quarantine, coming, as he did, from Pensacola, where there was yellow fever raging. As soon as Capt. J—— could recover from his astonishment, he, somewhat sarcastically, reminded Gen. Butler that he was a *naval* officer, under the command of an officer of the navy near at hand, to whom he was amenable, and that Flag Officer Farragut would probably be the person proper for him to complain to.

In a rage, Gen. Butler sent a communication to Farragut, asking "if the quarantine laws were to be obeyed."

"Certainly," replied the admiral.

"Then," wrote the autocrat, "the Tennessee having violated the quarantine, and having communicated with the other vessels, the whole squadron is hereby placed in quarantine and will communicate only with the flagship, which will be permitted to use the landing at the foot of Canal street only."

The unparalleled assurance shown in placing the fleet, upon which the safety of the city solely depended, the rebels having 30,000 men at Camp Moore, only a few miles distant, in quarantine, was immense.

Farragut, was, however, equal to the occasion, and calmly acquiesced as to the quarantine, but added that the proper place to ride out a quarantine would be at the quarantine grounds, thirty miles below the city.

Gen. Butler at once hastened to withdraw his demand, not being quite sure but that he would have reached the quarantine station himself, at about the same time with Farragut, had the squadron been sent away from New Orleans for as much as twenty-four hours.

I was once attached to a vessel that anchored in the harbor of Funchal, Madeira, and the first thing we did, when we got ashore, was to take a horseback ride round that beautiful island.

Some of the men had liberty also, and, of course, every one of them captured a horse as soon as they got fairly ashore. About half way up the mountain we came across a little mizzen topman, flushed and evidently very warm, riding a spirited little horse, with a stone tied up in a silk handkerchief slung to his tail.

The first lieutenant laughed and said:

"What are you doing with that handkerchief, Brown?"

"Why, you see, sir," said Brown, "that when I first hitched her up she pitched badly, being too much by the head, so I just rigged this stone on aft and brought her down to her bearings, and she sails now like a clipper, sir."

7

LETTER X.

One afternoon, in the year 1862, the gunboat Scioto
was coming down the Mississippi River on her way
to New Orleans. As she turned the bend near
Donaldsonville a battery of field artillery opened on
her, together with a fire of small arms from some
troops.

AN ENGAGEMENT.

The Scioto rounded to promptly and returned the
fire with her eleven-inch shell gun, her rifled Parrot
and twenty-four pound howitzer, and succeeded in
driving off the attacking party, but did not escape
without loss herself. A six-pound shot struck the
executive officer, who was standing near the eleven-
inch gun, tearing off his arm and striking him in the
side and hip, causing his death in a few minutes.
One man lost an arm and one or two others were
wounded by splinters.

On the arrival of the Scioto at New Orleans I was

at once detached from the frigate Mississippi and ordered as executive officer in the place of the dead lieutenant whom I knew so well. When the body was taken to the steamer for transportation to his home in Massachusetts, two lines of boats from the different ships of the squadron, forming a procession nearly half a mile in length, testified to the ready sympathy shown to a brave gentleman, by his associates, in the only way left to them.

We were on this

GUERRILLA DUTY,

up and down the river for nearly a year, and I assure you we were kept busy. One day we were protecting a steamer taking sugar at a plantation. The squad of soldiers went out, as usual, toward the sugar house, were surprised by guerrillas, the morning being foggy, and shot down. We heard the shots and opened fire in the direction, and by good luck, sent a shell right in the midst of the band, though invisible to us on account of the dense fog. We brought in the corporal of the party, who, with another wounded by the guerrilla shots, had hidden in a cane-field. The corporal stated that they were searching for him and would have got him, but that our shell came right in amongst them and drove them off.

EPILEPTIC OFFICERS.

On another occasion I was just ready to go on shore, with a party, to see if I could find a couple of howitzers that we heard the rebels had mounted in the neighborhood. I called to the acting master, who was to accompany me, to know if he had the rat-tail files to spike the guns with, if necessary. He turned to answer me, when I observed his features working convulsively, and down he went in an epileptic fit. I skirmished round on shore for an hour or two, but did not find any signs of guns. Just then I heard a shout, and hastening over to the other end of my skirmish-line, found the captain of the forecastle in an epileptic fit. Well, it took six men to hold him and bring him on board, and as I had only six left I concluded to let the guns go, and returned to the ship.

The acting master was the caterer of the ward-room mess, and not long after, while returning in the market boat, having been on shore to buy chickens, eggs, etc., he fell over in another fit, which lasted him a week before he was fully sane again.

One day while he was still confined to his room, we picked up

A BIG OWL

struggling in the river, and the idea occurred to me to play a joke on F—— when he came on deck again. So I prepared everybody, and when F—— came up

one morning, he asked where we were. I pointed to
the city, and said:

" Bâton Rouge."

He looked at me doubtfully, as we had never been
up so far before, and said:

" Sure ? "

" Certainly," said I, " that is Bâton Rouge, but," I
said, turning to the old owl, who at once rose upon
tip-toe, spread his wings wide, and opened his mouth,
" F——, that is a pretty way to squander our mess
money, to go ashore and give fifty cents and a half
plug of tobacco for that old owl, and bring it on
board for a turkey."

F—— looked at me incredulously and then at the
owl, who at once executed his pleasant little grimace
again, and walked forward without saying a word.
I saw him asking, evidently, if that was Bâton Rouge,
and then pointing to the owl, and as both answers
corroborated with my remarks, he was evidently
staggered. He took the first opportunity to throw
the owl overboard, but never alluded to the turkey,
and I don't think he ever knew, for certain, whether
he bought that owl or not.

We had

A VERY SMART CAT

on board who, having always been petted, was afraid
of nothing. He came up cautiously to a couple of rab-

bits one day, and would sit up and stroke their ears with his paw, being evidently much amused .to see them jump.

During owl week he had discovered the owl sitting on a cleat near the quarter deck, and prowled round to see what it was. He finally got quite near to Mrs. Owl, and sitting up, was about to stroke her ear, I guess, when suddenly the owl rose upon her toes, standing nearly three feet high, spread out her wings, and blinking rapidly, opened her mouth. Tom turned a series of back somersaults, and with his back arched double and tail of same thickness as his body, he took up a position on the hammock rail, and swore at the owl for five minutes.

THEY WANTED PORK.

One day we made a raid on a plantation and captured a lot of horses, mules, sheep, pigs, turkeys and geese, and took them over to Donaldsonville for the benefit of the troops there, keeping some mutton and poultry and a couple of pigs for ourselves. As there was so much poultry the captain directed the paymaster not to serve out any allowance of salt pork to the men, thinking that, of course, they would be much pleased with the substitute. At 12 o'clock, noon, there was a deputation of men at the mast "to know if they couldn't have their ration of pork that belonged to 'em, as half the men didn't want to eat them fresh water things (geese)."

Sailors are always willing to accept any little extras, but not at the expense of a single thing that belongs to them.

THAT PIG OF OURS.

We had kept for our own use two pigs, and they were suffered to run loose about the decks.

About six bells (3 P. M.), there was a commotion forward, and a man ran aft, to the officer of the deck, to report that one of the pigs was overboard and making for the shore. Away went two boats in pursuit, confident that they would pick him up in a moment, and bring him on board, but they reckoned without their pig, a host in himself. Just as the bow oarsman would reach down to grab him, piggy would dive and come up on the other side of the boat, amid the peals of laughter from the ship. The boats would back water, give way port, back starboard, stern all, then pull like blazes, but in vain, and it was not until piggy was exhausted, that they managed to get a line round his neck and haul him in.

When we went down to the blockade off Galveston, piggy accompanied us, and ate impartially at every mess in the ship. Old Charley Brown, a contraband, had him in special charge, and promptly resented any indignity offered to the pig. I remember one day

Charley came up in a rage, because the men were laughing to see the pig slide backward and forward across the deck, from one scupper to the other, as the ship rolled heavily, and did not offer to help his *protégé*. Charley promptly choked the luff of the pig with a big damp swab so he could remain quiet, notwithstanding the motion of the ship. As we were keeping an armed watch, and every eye on the alert, old Charley would march up and down during the mid-watch, with a pike over his shoulder, with which he would now and then make dashes at the hammock rail, to repel any imaginary boarders who might come over, the pig, trotting gravely at his heels, only making an occasional *detour* round the engine room hatch by way of a flier. Finally, through stress of hunger, we were compelled to kill the pig. Charley refused to do it, intimating that misfortune would certainly follow it, and on the evening following, in his French patois, he told me confidentially, that the pig had appeared to him and marched up and down the deck with him as usual.

"Do you believe in ghosts?"
he asked, and I was forced to admit that I did. Charley was consistent, and refused to eat a morsel of the fresh pork furnished by his old friend.

IMPUDENCE.

One of our vessels on the South Pacific station, was ordered by the admiral, to go to one of the Pacific Islands.

Well, the captain didn't want to go at all, so he waited until he was notified sharply to obey the order.

Not having gone on the day following, the fleet captain came on board, and said that the admiral's order was, "that if he was not under weigh by 12 o'clock, he would relieve him of his command, and prefer charges against him." So about 10 minutes of 12 he got under weigh, and started, but before he got two miles he made signal to the admiral, asking permission to "part company."

Squadron rules, "that no vessel shall part company with the flagship, except by permission," is a good thing, but the very impudence of his signal, after being almost kicked out, made it very funny.

PLAYING BOTH BOWERS.

A great many years ago one of our sloops of war was in the straits of Magellan, when it became necessary to anchor. The irascible commander was giving orders himself, and called out sharply,

"A hand by the starboard anchor."

The executive officer gently asked if it would not

be well to get a cast of the lead, to see how deep the water was first.   Annoyed at his evident mistake, the obstinate old fellow bellowed out:

"*No*, sir; let go the starboard anchor, sir," and away she went.   Each bower anchor has 150 fathoms, 900 feet of chain, and *this* chain skipped out lively; when it came to the bitter end, which is lashed to a bolt in the kelson, there was a wrench, and the last section, like a huge snake, writhed out at the hawse-hole in a shower of sparks.

"The anchor is *down*, sir," called out the officer of the forecastle cheerfully.

"A hand by the port anchor," shouted the captain, and the port anchor with its 900 feet of chain went down like a fiery serpent, in search of the starboard one.

There being no more anchors handy, the commander yielded charge of the deck to a less expensive subordinate, better acquainted with the lay of the land, who succeeded, after bending the sheet chains, in anchoring the ship to a better advantage.

ON THE BANKS OF NEWFOUNDLAND.

"Oh, captain, what are we stopping for?"

"Fog."

"But, captain, its clear overhead."

"Ain't going that way."

"Oh, captain, is it *always* foggy here?"

"How in the devil do I know, *I* don't *live* here?"

LETTER XI

THE SCIOTO OFF GALVESTON—WATCHING FOR A SAIL—
ORDERED TO PASS THE BATTERIES—THE HATTERAS
CHASES THE ALABAMA—AND THE ALABAMA SINKS
HER—THE PAYMASTER'S OMELET—A STICKLER
FOR RANK—HE FOUND THE MAN WHO FURNISHED
THE CHEESE—A ROLLING GUNBOAT.

The Scioto was for some six months on the blockade

OFF GALVESTON, TEXAS.

There was a good deal of rivalry between the gunboats as to which should report first that a sail was
in sight. So in order to stimulate our mast-head
lookouts to watchfulness I had given directions that
if our lookout reported a sail *first*, he would be
relieved at once, but if the lookout of a rival gunboat got ahead of him he was to be kept up there all
day. Thanks to this competitive system, we were
generally the first to report a sail.

ALWAYS READY.

The steam was kept low with the fires banked; the
chain brought to the capstan, with the anchor just

under foot, ready to trip at a moment's notice, and orders given, so that at the cry of,

"Sail ho ! "

from the mast-head, the men sprang to the bars and commenced to heave round, the engineer spread his fires, the quartermaster bent on the signal number 1258, which telegraphed to the flagship,

"Strange sail to the eastward,"

and as soon as answered up went interrogatory 896, meaning,

"Can I give chase ?"

The captain came up at once, and in *one minute* from the discovery, the ship was under weigh, standing out to sea.

One Saturday the commodore announced that on Monday, if pleasant, we would

ATTEMPT TO PASS THE BATTERIES

and enter Galveston; so we were all feeling correspondingly uncomfortable, not, of course, because we were *afraid* at all—in fact we were the original parties who were "longing for the fray," men of gore, whose trade was war and rapine, more particularly, perhaps, the latter. Still we were familiar with the reputation of the Texas riflemen as marksmen, and we knew there were a good many chances in favor of some losing the number of their mess, and leaving

their families unprovided for; some of us were even
not insured, so reckless had we become, inured to toil
and danger as we were, bronzed by the tropic sun for,
say, three or four months.

Well, we looked up our little matters, some of us
had our hair cut; others hunted up their bibles,
which were safely stowed away in their lockers, and
all wore a pretty serious air, I assure you. Sunday
was a delightful day, and the prospect that Monday
would be pleasant was very good, or rather, very
bad, indeed.

About 4 p. m. we observed that

THE HATTERAS WAS UNDER WEIGH,

with signal,

"Strange sail to the eastward,"
flying. I accordingly doomed our unfortunate lookout to stay up there until sunset for not seeing it
first; as it turned out, I have forgotten whether he
was ultimately rewarded for it or not. As the Hatteras steamed off in pursuit, having permission from
the flagship so to do, she signaled,

"Strange sail suspicious,"
and later,

"Strange sail positively an enemy,"
soon after disappearing in pursuit. Let me say here
that this last signal was not understood at the time.

About dusk (say 7 P. M.), as the captain and myself were pacing the quarter deck, we noted flashes of heat lightning, as we thought, to the eastward, but soon a low thunder which followed led us to believe that it was firing of great guns. We timed the flash and report, and estimated the distance to be twenty miles, allowing 1,120 feet per second for the velocity of sound.

The captain at once took his gig and went on board the flagship, leaving me to get the ship under weigh. After some delay the flagship Brooklyn, the Katahdin, and the Scioto were standing out to sea, in pursuit. Well, we steamed until 1 A. M., and finding nothing the Katahdin and Scioto returned to their anchorage.

THE HATTERAS SUNK BY THE ALABAMA.

About 7 A. M. the next morning a white whale boat was seen approaching the ship from the shore. We watched it with considerable curiosity, as we supposed it to be another flag of truce from the "rebs." As it dashed up alongside it proved to be the Hatteras's gig. The acting master in charge came on board and touched his cap, and answered my question of,

"Where is the Hatteras, sir?"
with,

"The Hatteras was sunk at 7.30 last evening, sir, by the 290."

"Walk down in the cabin, sir, and report to the captain,"
I said, and giving directions to drop the boat astern, and let the crew come aboard to breakfast, I was obliged to await the result of his interview with the captain, anxious as I was to learn the particulars. The crew of the boat were the center of attraction forward, and our men soon knew as much as they did.

We at once got under weigh, and put to sea in pursuit of the Brooklyn. As soon as she saw us she came after us, under full steam, hoping that we were the Alabama, and seemed correspondingly disgusted upon discovering our true character. Upon comparing notes we found that the Brooklyn had picked up two of the Hatteras's boats, lashed together, with clothing in them stained with blood, and that she discovered the Hatteras, sunk in nine fathoms, with her mastheads sticking out of water, where she now is, I suppose.

A SHORT FIGHT, BUT A HOT ONE.

We afterwards learned that Capt. Blake was positive in his mind that the vessel he was approaching was the Alabama; he had his cutlass ground sharp, and determined to run down his enemy, far his superior in force, and carry him by boarding.

As he approached he hailed,

"What vessel is that?"

"Her Britannic Majesty's ship Spitfire," was the reply, at the same time running up the English flag.

"I'll send a boat aboard of you," said the Hatteras's captain.

"Aye, aye, sir,"
was the reply, and as the gig approached her the Alabama lowered her ladder, and showed a light over the side, it being just dusk.

At this exciting moment the captain of the Alabama called out:

"This is the 290,"
and bang! went his broadside into the Hatteras, down came the English flag and up went the Stars and Bars.

The Hatteras replied nobly and struck the Alabama twenty-two times with her shot and shell.

The shot of the Alabama, however, soon pierced her thin iron hull, and penetrating her boilers rendered her helpless, enveloped in a cloud of steam, the Alabama steaming round in a circle pouring in shot and shell.

Finding it impossible to do else, Capt. Blake surrendered and transferred his crew to the Alabama just in time to escape the going down of the Hatteras. The Alabama at once steamed off to the eastward, and plunging into the darkness was soon beyond pursuit.

Capt. Semmes remarked that he didn't want to fight any more men-of-war, as he suffered considerably with his fight with the Hatteras, but he did try it again off the coast of France, and was sunk by the United States steamer Kearsarge in a fight of two hours, escaping himself in the English yacht Deerhound, which by some peculiar notion of neutrality picked him up and ran off with him.

"It is an ill wind that blows nobody good," is a true proverb. By the loss of the Hatteras we were too weak to attack the Galveston forts, and the attack was postponed. Hence these tales.

AN EGG STORY.

One day our commander happened to be on board the flagship, when an officer came on board from shore with a flag of truce. While waiting to be shown into the cabin the officer recognized in him an old class and shipmate. They shook hands and gossiped a while, and, upon leaving the ship, the "reb" offered to send our skipper a couple of dozen of eggs. When the eggs arrived the commander sent a half dozen down into the wardroom to the paymaster.

8

Well, Pay was delighted. Eggs was *eggs* just then, as we had lived on our rations for the last three months; so he bragged about his eggs until the rest of the mess were dissolved in envy. The following morning, at breakfast, an omelet was placed in front of the paymaster which certainly contained, at least, five eggs. The paymaster was furious.

"Steward! where's the steward?" he shouted.

While the boy went forward after the steward, Pay regarded the omelet gloomily, and coldly invited each member of the mess to take some. All declined save two, who ate with great satisfaction the portion allotted them. Notwithstanding his evident annoyance, Pay commenced to eat some of the omelet, when the steward appeared with a covered dish in his hands.

"Steward!" shouted the paymaster, "what in the d——l do you mean by cooking all of those eggs at once? Besides, I told you I wanted 'em boiled."

"Here's your eggs, sir," said the unruffled steward, uncovering the dish and setting five eggs down on the table, "one of 'em was bad."

A smile broke over the face of the paymaster, and after finishing the omelet and offering the boiled eggs to each, he reached out and took one himself. He looked at it curiously, and with a muttered swear he dashed it down, and rising from the table, rushed on deck.

I did not understand, but managed to gather from the explanation furnished by one of the omelet eaters, interrupted by frequent laughter, that he and the other confederate had sat up half the night blowing out the contents of the eggs with straws through small orifices; the result of the blowing was made into omelet, and the shells being boiled filled with water, and for a moment deceived a person into taking one.

I was real glad that I did not take omelet with mine. The missing sixth egg was accounted for by the blower's stating that in his haste and fear of detection, he had dropped it on the wardroom floor. It might have appeared at breakfast, however, as a dropped egg, but didn't.

Every day or two after the paymaster would burst into the wardroom in a rage because some allusion to eggs had been dropped.

AN OFFICER OVERBOARD.

They tell the story of the eccentric old captain. now dead, formerly in command of the North Carolina. He was a martinet and very profane. On one occasion he fell overboard in crossing the gangway plank from the cobb dock to the ship. The sentry in the gangway promptly called out:

"Man overboard!"

"An officer, you blasted fool!"

spluttered the captain, as he rose to the surface for the second time,

"An officer, sir."

NO CHANCE FOR THE WINNER.

The same captain bantered the executive officer of the ship into a wager to race with him, the former having, as he supposed, a crack boat and crew.

The race came off, but the irascible commander, seeing that he was being badly beaten, made the surrounding air blue with his sulphurous oaths, while executing a war dance in the stern of his boat, ordered the other to,

"Lay on his oars,"

and, upon their return to the ship, put the executive officer under arrest for disrespect to his superior and commanding officer in *daring* to pass the former without permission.

There is nothing to show that the captain ever paid the bet, but the ship's log records the fact that not long after the executive officer was transferred to a sea-going ship, where racing boats to win, could be more profitably engaged in with safety to the leading boat.

JUST THE MAN HE WANTED.

An old man-of-warsman took his seat in a passenger car one day, attracting some considerable attention by his dress and manner. One of those meddlesome sort of people, described in that laughable book "On Wheels," moved over, and took a seat alongside the sailor.

"In the navy, eh?"

The sailor nodded affirmatively.

"Well," said the interlocutor hesitatingly, "I am not *exactly in* the navy myself. I am a contractor—that is, I furnish cheese to the navy."

"Oh! you *are*, are ye?" said the sailor menacingly. "you are just the chap I've been looking for."

And accordingly he knocked the aspirant for naval honors over the car seat, and added, as he looked inquiringly up, and down the car,

"Now show me the son-of-a-gun that furnishes butter."

A ROLLING GUNBOAT.

"Twice ten tempestuous nights I rolled, resigned
To roaring billows and the warring wind."

The Scioto rolled terribly, when in the trough of the sea, to the great detriment of our crockery; though we always had sand bags lashed round the rim of the table to save the pieces. I have seen an officer vibrate between the table and the bulk-head holding a plate of soup in his hands, his chair slipping back and forth over the smooth oil cloth of the ward room floor.

One of our officers, returning from a visit, said, admiringly,

"That New London is a bully little steamer."

" Why ? "

"Because she rolls so confounded fast that the dishes don't have time to slip off the table."

I have heard an old sailor yarn, where a schooner, *he* was in, rolled *clear over* one night, and so easy, too, that they'd never have known it, but that every man had a *round turn in his hammock clews.*

LETTER XII.

"Now on their coasts our conquering navy rides,
Waylays their merchants, and their land besets."

THE BLOCKADE OFF GALVESTON — A LITTLE BATTERY
PRACTICE — "HE WHO FIGHTS AND," ETC. — IN A
VERY SERIOUS PREDICAMENT — WHY THE CAPTAIN
"SET 'EM UP FOR THE BOYS" — HOW THE CAP-
TAIN WAS SHOT IN THE NECK — THE REBEL RAM
ARKANSAS RUNS THE GAUNTLET — THE PHILOSO-
PHY OF DESERTION—THE RETORT DISCOURTEOUS—
IN THE IRISH CHANNEL.

While on the blockade, off Galveston, the gunboats
used to get under weigh at daylight, and run down
to the flag-ship for company, returning to their
stations just after dark. This enabled the officers to
visit one another during the day, and tended to mis-
lead the rebels as to where we lay during the night.
Had we selected any particular anchorage, it would
have been easy for blockade runners to have run in
by a route far enough away from the gunboats to
have escaped observation in the darkness; and again,
a permanent anchorage might have enabled a ram to
come out some pleasant, obscure evening, and sink a
gunboat or two.

DRAWING THE ENEMY'S FIRE.

One afternoon we steamed slowly in toward Galveston, and threw some shell into the city, aimed at the captured steamer Harriet Lane, which lay at a wharf inside. We succeeded in having her towed away up the bay, and also succeeded in drawing the fire of the shore battery near by, as well as fire from Fort Point, some two and a half miles distant.

I remember looking through the glass, trying to see the battery, as located by the captain, when a shot came whistling just over us; and, do you know, that I could not get a focus on that glass to save me, and it was a good glass, too. The long shots from the batteries on the Point were

TRYING TO THE NERVES,

I assure you, on account of the time elapsing between the puff of smoke and the arrival of the shot; the time was probably only ten seconds, but if a fellow was dancing around you with a big club, and you were waiting for him to hit you most anywhere, you wasn't sure where, time would be time. A puff of white smoke would shoot out from the fort, and we knew that something was coming. After a while you would hear a murmuring sound, like the wind in a distant grove, growing deeper and fuller, until, like the blast of a hurricane, it rushed over and struck the water near by, throwing a column fifty feet into the air, simultaneously relieving the suspended respiration of 150 sets of lungs, whose owners were earning their living literally by the sweat of their brows. Well, we just put our little helm a-starboard. and dusted out of that, a parting shot throwing the spray quite on board, and having the extraordinary effect of increasing the revolutions of the screw to a maximum.

After dark we got under weigh, to go to our anchorage for the night, and steamed off to the northward and eastward.

As we approached Fort Point, the captain thought he would explore the channel a little, and stood close in toward the fort. Suddenly, with an easy grating slide, the little steamer was

HARD AND FAST AGROUND.

As the fellow who asked for gape seed, in New York, would say, we backed her, and we backed her. and we backed her; and we rolled her, and rolled her, and rolled her; for two hours we worked to try and get her off, without success. We sent a boat to the flagship for assistance; got a heavy kedge out with a hawser to the capstan, and backed her and rolled her again, but to no purpose.

The captain then gave me orders to throw over the

coal, and to lighten the ship as best I could. I asked
for one more trial before throwing away coal that
was worth, down there, $20 a ton in gold, and he
consented to hold on a little longer. You can
imagine that we were anxious to get out of there
before daylight revealed our position to the batteries
not a mile distant, and as the daylight would bring
us certain demolition, we cast an anchor out of the
stern of the ship, and *dreaded* the day.

OFF AT LAST.

I stationed every man in the ship along the starboard side, and made them a little speech, and at the
order

"Rush,"

they rushed violently over to the port side; again the
"rush" order, and back went every son of 'em,
laughing, as if it were a good joke. Then we
manned the capstan again and walked away with
the hawser. The man in the chains quietly watched
his lead, and reported no movement; the engines
were backing all they knew how; the quartermaster
reported quietly,

"The kedge is coming home, sir;"

round went the capstan.

"Heave and walk him up, bullies," I said, "and
we'll back the kedge and try again."

Just them the kedge tripped under the stern, the ship swung back to port and slowly moved; the imperturbable leadsman in the chains remarking quietly,

"She's going astern, sir;"

and, sure enough, she was. As soon as I had her safely clear, I sent down word to the captain, and after we were safely anchored he embraced me warmly, invited us all down in the cabin and "set 'em up for the boys."

THE CAPTAIN'S WOUND.

The same gunboat was before this time at Vicksburg and was ordered, with others of the squadron, to pass the batteries and come down the river.

The vessels were exposed to a very severe fire and suffered considerably, being struck several times.

One shot struck the carriage of the rifle gun on the forecastle, knocked over several of the crew, killing one man instantly, and altogether it was pretty warm work. About this time the captain was coming aft, and was passing the engine room hatch, when a shell struck in the water ways and exploded with a terrific noise in a chicken coop, distributing some twenty chickens and ducks impartially over the ship: a good chunk of chicken, or duck, I won't be sure which, struck the captain in the back of the neck;

as the warm blood trickled down his back, he, suppos-
ing that he was mortally wounded, or worse, walked
slowly aft, holding his hands a little out from his
side, as a person would who was afraid his spine
would drop out, and while reflecting on some appropriate last words, such as "Don't give up the fight,"
or "Bury me in the salt, salt sea" (then a thousand miles distant), was surprised and pleased when
the quartermaster, who was wiping off his neck,
assured him that he was not wounded. The captain
takes much more pleasure in telling his story to-day,
than he would if it had turned out differently.

A few days before this

THE REBEL RAM ARKANSAS

suddenly came out of the Yazoo River and passed
down in broad daylight, right through the squadron
lying at anchor. It was a clean surprise. She had
been built up a narrow stream and we had no suspi-
cion that there was such a vessel.

As she passed down, every vessel that could bring
a gun to bear, fired at her, but without effect, as
she had closed her ports and her heavily iron-
cladded hull was impervious to their shot.

It was evident that she would pass quite near the
Scioto, and active preparations were made to give
her a warm reception. The shell was quickly drawn

from the eleven-inch gun and a solid shot substituted. As the dangerous craft appeared the gun was brought to bear, and the breech raised so as to hit her at the water line. Now she was right abreast.

"Lower a little more,"
was the order, and the instant that was to immortalize the Scioto and shed glory upon the officers, "the tide that was in the affairs of gunboats to lead them on to fortune," seemed embodied in that instant.

"Fire,"
was upon the lips of the captain, when a little roll to starboard started the shot in the gun, and it rolled miserably out at the muzzle, and dropped ingloriously into the water.

The loader, in his haste, had forgotten to put a grommet wad over the shot. The commanding officer sat down on a spit-box and buried his face in his hands; every one looked every way for Sunday, not to see the grief stamped upon the countenances of all hands, and all hands would have been willing to have stamped upon the unhappy loader, had he not prudently withdrawn himself. I have never learned what became of the loader. I suppose he wanders to and fro upon the face of the earth a victim to "what might have been."

THE FASCINATION OF DESERTION.

"Captain," said a lady to an old sailor who had commanded many ships, "can you tell me why the men desert so much? Is it because they are ill-treated?"

"Well, no, not exactly," replied the man of experience. "Sometimes they are ill-treated, but again, they will desert where they are well treated. In fact, madam," said he, warming to his subject, "judging from the little experience I've had with sailor men (he had been going to sea, man and boy, for forty years), I really believe that if you freighted a ship for heaven, and was obliged to touch in at hell for wood and water, half the boat's crew would desert."

HOW I LOST MY ARM.

There is a story which is such a good joke on myself, that I hasten to tell it before some one else does. I was returning invalided from New Orleans, having reached Cairo in the Black Hawk, Admiral Porter's flagship, and had taken the train for Cincinnati. On the train was a private soldier, evidently just discharged, noisy and familiar with his superiors in rank, being as good as any colonel or major, etc. I saw that he had been drinking, and I had taken a dislike to him from his action in the train.

On our arrival at Odin we found that we had

missed connection and would have to stay all night; the beds were all taken and I stood leaning against the wall of the office, cogitating as to what I should do, being almost helpless, when up came my soldier and asked roughly and impertinently,

" Where did you lose your arm ?"

I looked him full in the face and in a tone replete with dignity (that was my idea) intended to crush his impertinence, replied. "I was hit with a club in the Mexican war, sir."

"Oh, you were, eh," he said sneeringly, "it's a pity it didn't knock your d—d head off."

That man, I have reason to believe, still lives.

IN THE IRISH CHANNEL.

"Are you sure of the channel, pilot?" asked an anxious captain as the ship seemed to be getting very near shore.

"Shure, is it? bedad, captain, darlin', I know every rock in ould Ireland," and, as just then the ship struck heavily,

"I'm a Dutchman ef there ain't wan of thim."

LETTER XIII.

"He like a foolish pilot, hath shipwreck'd
My vessel gloriously rigged."

A FRUITLESS CHASE OFF GALVESTON—MAN OVERBOARD
—A COLLISION ON THE MISSISSIPPI RIVER—HEAVE
ROUND.

THE ROCKET.

One beautiful evening while lying at anchor on the blockade, off Galveston, a rocket was suddenly seen to seaward.

"Stand by to slip,"

called the officer of the deck;

"Boy, tell the engineer to spread fires,"

"Slip, go ahead, one bell,"

and in five seconds we were standing out to sea, all hands excited, and hoping that it would prove to be a blockade runner worth a *million* dollars. As we passed the Itasca, her commander called out:

"What is it, L——?"

"A rocket to seaward," replied the skipper, "come along."

"All right,"

was the reply, and soon the Itasca was steaming up alongside, and was shortly lost to view on our starboard bow.

The night was clear, with only a light breeze blowing, the sea was smooth, the moon shone brightly, and as I stood on the ship's rail, leaning on the boarding netting, I thought, well, there *is* a bright side to even blockading; what a lovely night, and how easily the little Scioto runs her ten knots an hour; no sea on, no motion; if we could only have it this way always. Suddenly the cry,

"MAN OVERBOARD,"

rudely dispelled my contemplation of the beauties of the sea, and the bright side of blockading.

"Stop her,"

"Three bells, a turn back;"

"Away there, life-boat's crew, clear away the gig," I sang out as I jumped, and let go the life-buoy myself. The gig was lowered, the men sliding down the falls and tumbling into the boat.

"Pull right astern and keep the lights in range," I said. as, by the captain's orders, the quartermaster hoisted a light forward, and the gig plunged into the darkness, and was soon far astern. By keeping the ship headed as she was when the man fell overboard, and hoisting range lights forward and aft, the gig would, of course, be able to pull back exactly over the track made by the ship, and must pass close to the man, if afloat.

" Who was it ? "
was the question next asked.

" Old Rogers, sir, the gunner's mate," answered the
captain of the forecastle; "he leaned against one of
the pivot ports, sir, and it dropped down, sir, and he
went overboard."

" Yes, sir," said the man in the chains, " and I hove
the lead-line right between his hands, and he couldn't
catch it, sir."

Pretty soon the gig returned with the life-buoy and
the mournful report:

" We couldn't see nothing of him, sir."

" Hook your boat on.   Lay aft to the gig's falls,"
was the order, and the men silently hoisted the boat,
and off went the Scioto again in pursuit of the
rocket.

True, she was short a hand, but then you know if
the rocket proved to be an enemy, and showed fight,
why we would probably be short more than one.

INSPIRATION FOR AN ARTIST.

I often think of that scene, and wish that a painter
could have stood with me on the rail of that steamer
—the painting of it would eclipse any marine view
ever yet exhibited.   The gig had just pulled off
astern, the quartermasters standing on the stern rail
of the ship burning Coston's signals, illuminating the
sea for a mile round, and as the bright flame now

green, now red, lighted up the eager faces of the crew, all crowding and gazing aft, alternately with a ghastly pallor and rosy light, the ship rising and falling easily on the long swell of the Gulf of Mexico, with every thread of rigging standing out bright on the dark background of the sky, it was a most beautiful picture.

HUNTING IN COUPLES.

The Scioto and Itasca were ninety-day gun-boats, or, as they were called, the 23's: they carried an eleven-inch pivot gun amidships, a twenty-pounder rifle Parrot on the topgallant forecastle, and four howitzers aft. By an arrangement with the Itasca, we were to hunt in couples, the Scioto fighting her starboard battery, and the Itasca her port battery. By this means we could pivot our heavy eleven-inch to starboard and carry it athwartships ready for use, instead of securing it fore and aft, as was the usual custom.

It was the duty of

THE GUNNER'S MATE

to see that the pivot ports were hauled up, and stopped only with a yarn, so that in case we had to use the gun suddenly, the ports could be instantly dropped and the gun fired at once. On this fatal evening, he had secured the ports as usual, reporting the same to the officer of the deck at eight P. M., and forgetting what he had done, leaned against one of them, which giving way, plunged him into the water; being an old man and incumbered in a heavy pea-coat, he was unable to keep up.

He had been in the navy all his life, and used to tell how he was on board the brig Somers when young Spencer was hanged for mutiny.

Well, we ran on until about midnight, and still saw nothing to explain the rocket. Up came the Itasca, and sneeringly asked:

"WHERE'S YOUR BLOCKADE RUNNER?"

so we concluded to just keep steerage way on and let the watch turn in, all hands having been on deck all the evening, and wait for daylight.

I lay down in my clothes, with my sword and revolver in my belt, and went to sleep. It seemed as if I had only about closed my eyes, when whir-r-r went the rattle, and I climbed on deck in a hurry, I tell you.

The captain met me at the head of the ladder, and with a stage whisper, led me forward by the pivot gun; I stooped down at his bidding and looked.

"What do you think of it?" he whispered anxiously.

"Think?" said I, "it's the Great Eastern."

Just then along came our old friend, the Itasca; we pointed out the steamer, and then both started for her, the Itasca on her starboard hand and we on the port. Well, the Itasca was the fastest, and darted ahead. We approached the steamer cautiously, when, suddenly there was a rushing sound from forward, and the officer of the forecastle sang out:

"Hard a-port; quick's your play."

We jammed down our helm, when whiz went the Itasca past us, running about ten knots. She had made the circuit of the steamer, and coming back we narrowly escaped a collision that would have sunk one or both of us.

A DISAPPOINTMENT.

Well, our rocket was only a friend, another man-of-war, come to join the squadron, and he had concluded to anchor for the night when we discovered him. We all stood in for our anchorage, and passed close under the stern of the flagship about 7.30 in the morning. The commodore was on deck, and he hailed us with:

"Good morning, captain. What vessel is that?"

"The United States steamer B——," was the reply.

"How did you know she was out there, sir?"

"Saw her signals about 8.30 last evening; been out after her all night, sir,"
answered our captain.

As we steamed slowly over to our anchorage, I saw the commodore pulling some hair out of his chin whiskers and gesticulating to an unhappy quartermaster, and I thanked my stars that I didn't have the first watch last night aboard the flagship.

ON A SINKING GUN-BOAT.

One bright June day the Scioto entered the Southwest Pass, Mississippi River, and taking a pilot, steamed up the river, bound for New Orleans for repairs, and a hospital for me.

I was lying in a cot just under the ward-room hatch outside my state-room. All hands were pleased to hear the news of the fall of Vicksburg, and looked forward to a pleasant visit to New Orleans after several months' blockading.

As we steamed steadily along, I became aware that we were approaching or meeting a steamer coming down the river. I heard the contradictory orders of the pilot,

"Starboard,"

"Port,"

"Steady,

some confusion, and then an easy grating sound and motion exactly like the gentle glide of a boat upon a sloping beach. The descending steamer struck us just abaft the forechains, cutting into us clear to the kelson. Soon I heard the master-at-arms come aft, and report,

"Five feet of water on the berthdeck, sir;"
some one else cried out,

"We are sinking."

The engines were started ahead again, and the ship was run ashore; the engineer came up and reported:

"The water is over the fire-room floor, sir,"
again,

"The fires are out, sir."

The engine pegged away a few minutes longer and then slowly stopped, and the impassible chief engineer came up and reported:

"The engines have stopped, sir."

(We had a fussy sort of officer at the Naval Academy, when I was a midshipman, and the cadets said he liked the evening gun because it always *reported* when it went off.)

The doctor then came down, and had me carried on deck in my cot, and put into one of the quarter boats. (They were about to lower the boat with the crew in her, but I knew that the eye bolts in the bow and stern would not hold, and I made the men get out, as I feared a plunge in the Mississippi would not help me any in my somewhat weak condition.)

I was put safely on board the steamer which ran into us, which turned out to be the Antona, a cap-

tured blockade runner, now a store-ship. About
dark a tug came along, and I started for New
Orleans where I arrived at daylight the next morning.

The Scioto sunk to her spar deck, and the men and
officers spent the night on deck with the mosquitoes,
being taken off and sent to New Orleans the next
day. The mosquitoes are so large on the banks of the
lower Mississippi, that they may be killed with a
shot-gun, sometimes.

I had quite comfortable quarters in the Army Hospital at New Orleans, it being previously the St.
James Hotel.

I received many calls, and presents of delicacies,
from the ladies of New Orleans, though very Confederate in their sentiments, and spent three weeks there
very comfortably. The Confederate ward was just
above me, and was well filled with wounded "rebs"
from Port Hudson. As the visitors to the Confederates had to pass my door, I made many acquaintances
among them, and as I have said received considerable
attention.

IF YOU CAN ONLY KEEP IT.

While lying at the New York Navy Yard one of
our men, a captain of the foretop, was returning
from liberty and coming down the wharf, bound for
the ship; the night being dark, he ran into a big man

in a heavy coat, who was coming in the opposite direction.

"Do you know who you are running into?" said the stranger.

"No, I don't," said the inebriated son of the sea, "and, what's more, I don't care a continental."

"Well, sir, I am Admiral ——, and I am in command of this yard."

"Well, admiral," said the unabashed man-of-wars-man, while remembrances of the ups and downs in his own checkered career on board ship flashed through his mind, "that's a mighty good billet if you can only *keep it.*"

HEAVE ROUND.

An old lady passing along the dock, saw some sailors on board of one of the lake schooners heaving up anchor. The anchor was up to the hawse-hole, but the men not noticing it, continued hauling, with a,

"Yah *heave* oh."

"Well!" said she, "you may 'Yah *heave* oh' just as much as ye like, but if you pull that crooked iron through that little hole in a hurry, I'm mistaken.

LETTER XIV.

"The plenteous board, high heap'd with cates divine,
And o'er the foaming bowl the laughing wine."

ON THE SOUTH PACIFIC STATION — AT CALLAO.

I happened to be navigator of the Tuscarora on the South Pacific Station in 1868, at the time of the great earthquake of that year, and think that some description might be of some interest to you.

When the Tuscarora came into the Bay of Callao, in latitude twelve degrees south, to report to the admiral commanding the squadron, there were several English, French and Peruvian men-of-war, as well as three or four of our own ships, lying at anchor.

Permission having been given us by signal to anchor, the commander of the Tuscarora, of course, called at once on the admiral, to report his arrival and receive orders as to the disposition of his ship. Upon his return he notified the executive officer that we would remain in Callao for a few days, and that the officers would be permitted to visit the shore.

NAVAL COURTESIES.

As is the custom, the officers of all the different ships came on board the next day to call and get acquainted, excepting the officers of the English frigate Topaz.

We promptly returned the visits of the Reindeers, L'Etoiles, Powhatans, Independencias and Huascars, but never went near the Topaz. Not long after some of our English naval friends laughingly told us that the Topaz officers said:

"That they daren't go near those Tuscarora fellows, you knaw; they's such blawsted swells, you knaw; they wear epaulets on Sundays and won't call on you unless you call first with your card turned down at every corner, you knaw."

We afterwards got well acquainted with the Topaz officers, and found them very jolly and pleasant fellows, indeed.

The climate of Callao seemed to me about the same all the year round, but the natives called the seasons by different names as do we. I never knew, however, after being on the station two and a half years, whether winter was in June or November.

I have a faint recollection of asking for grapes once in June, and being laughed at; being told that we had *oranges* in June but *grapes* in January.

I was very much astonished on going into a barber shop one day in Lima to get shaved, at being told by the barber, after shaving me, that I must get up and wash my own face.

In the shops you are expected to beat down the price always, until you are gravely assured that " *la ultima* " is reached, when you calmly pay the price and go.

I promptly informed one diamond seller that I was a North American, whereupon he apologized and gave me the lowest price at once.

One day, wishing a door-key made, I asked in Spanish,

" When can I have it ? "

The smith answered,

" Oh, Pasada Mañana ! " (Day after to-morrow.)

Noting his English accent, I said:

"I am an American, sir, when can I have the key ? "

"I beg your pardon, sir," said the Englishman, "I thought you were a Dago. Come in half an hour."

WARD-ROOM MESS.

There were twenty of us in the ward-room mess, the executive officer sitting at the forward end of the table, and the paymaster, who was the caterer, sitting at the after end, the line officers, that is lieutenants and masters, on the starboard side nearest their state-rooms, the staff officers, engineers, doctors and paymasters, on the port side. We had a very jolly mess, I assure you. Most of us had been on foreign stations, and we could relate various experiences and tell stories culled from every quarter of the world. We had lunch at 8 A. M., consisting of coffee, chocolate, toast, oranges, bananas, ripe figs, peeled and eaten with cream and powdered sugar; chiri-moyas, sweet, ripe and custardy, which you ate with a spoon, holding the fruit in your left hand; grenadillas, which left a seed wedged in between every tooth in your head, delicious pine-apples from Guayaquil (Y-a-keel), and grapes from Valparaiso (Vale of Paradise).

By 11 o'clock A. M., the most of the drills and exercises being over, we had a regular meat breakfast, "same as Melican man." At five P. M. we had a dinner of seven or eight courses, flanked with appropriate wines, and finished with a delightful Havana cigar.

We generally purchased wines for the wine mess, which is distinct from the ward-room mess, in Panama, which is a free port, and where the best could be bought, free of duty, and very cheap, and cigars in the same way.

There is a vague idea, prevalent in the minds of visitors on board a man-of-war, that the government pays for the entertainment furnished so freely to them; that there is a fund expressly provided by a benevolent Congress to buy whisky and cigars for the men, and light wines and biscuits for the women, when the Americans visit one of their ships.

It is a mistake; give the officer who entertains you credit for his hospitality, for he pays for what he orders, himself ; and, I can assure you, from actual experience, that hospitality as it is freely exercised on board ship, is costly, and forms a very considerable item in the expense account of a naval officer. In rare cases table money is allowed admirals for entertainment of royalty abroad, but the case is so rare that I do not know personally of a single one.

When a ship fits out for sea,

EACH MESS ELECTS A CATERER,

who takes charge of the mess matters and accounts; a vote is taken and generally results in assessing $100 apiece, outfit for crockery, table linen, etc., and $30 a month in advance each for mess bill.

The government furnishes servants, fires and lights only. The midshipmen mess by themselves, in the starboard steerage, and live in proportion to their means.

Frequently a midshipman dines in the cabin or in the ward-room by invitation; eats his own dinner religiously in the steerage first, borrows all the clothes of his messmates that he wants, oftener without permission than with, and enlarges at supper for the benefit of his envious shipmates upon what he had for dinner in the cabin. The wine !

"Jim, did you get any of that Madeira, when you dined in the cabin, that the skipper brought over himself?"

"I had three glasses and was going for another when old Beeswax asked me if the ship wasn't swinging, and I went on deck to tell the officer of the deck to tend her and not foul the anchor."

"THE JOLLY TUSCARORAS."

"He could on either side dispute.
Confute, change hands, and still confute."

Sometimes topics would fail at table, and every occasion was eagerly sought that would make talk; if a fellow said a thing was all colors, black, red, white. etc., he was quickly taken up by some argumentative cuss, who offered to bet him $5 that black was *not* a color, or he would take the opposite side and prove that black and white *were* colors.

It got so that they said aboard the other ships that an officer of the Tuscarora never came out of his state-room to breakfast and ventured the remark that it was a pleasant day, without first laying a $5 bill down by his plate in case it should be disputed.

Some visitors were on board one day and were admiring

THE NEATNESS OF THE SHIP,

the whiteness of the decks, and so forth, and walking forward were attracted by the extraordinary care

shown in the appearance of the pivot gun; the carriage was pure white, the bolts were jet black; the
gun, itself, coated with a lacquer of bees-wax and
blacking, was laboriously polished with corks until
you could see your face in it.   One of the ladies
admiringly passed her delicately gloved hand over
the smooth surface of the gun, and exclaimed,

"How glossy and smooth it is,"
to the great disgust of the old quarter gunner, who
muttered as the party turned away,

"They ain't satisfied to look at at a gun without
sticking their d——d dirty paws all over it."

THE MIDSHIPMEN

generally live like fighting cocks in port, and, from
dire necessity, on their rations when at sea, and frequent cruises are very necessary to compel the
improvident youngsters to save enough money at sea,
where they can't spend it, to carry them decently
through while in port.   It is such a nuisance for a
midshipman to have to pay out good money for his
daily bread, that the marrying of a girl *who can pay
her own mess bill*, is the universal foundation stone in
the Spanish castle of every incipient Nelson in the
service.

There is an idea that a naval officer, in addition to
his pay, gets a certain number of *rations*, which com-

muted, forms a handsome sum of money. This is not true. Each officer, petty officer, seaman, ordinary seaman, landsman or marine, receives *one* ration worth twenty-five cents per day, and in default of the spirit ration, which used to be issued (a tot of grog) twice a day, he receives five cents.

> "For they've raised his pay five cents a day,
> But stopped his grog forever."

Officers generally commute their ration, drawing the thirty cents a day in cash. The caterer of the mess is allowed to draw from the paymaster double the amount of the ration of any article allowed, by paying for it, provided that the men are not deprived thereby.

A GENIAL OLD COMMODORE.

One of our vessels lay at anchor in the Bay of Naples; the old commodore had quarantined every midshipman to the ship for some infraction of discipline. They hadn't their copy of the watch quarter and station bill, or the log written up, or they had neglected to work their "day's work" (of "dead reckoning"), perhaps; anyway the old scalawag had said that not a midshipman should leave the ship. Just as the 3 o'clock boat was called away a few of the youngsters were disconsolately walking up and down the port side of the quarter-deck, or peering

over the gangway, longingly looking ashore, trying
to "see Naples and not die," and furtively watching
the old commodore as he paced up and down the
deck.   Suddenly he stopped, and looking at the
victims, sternly said:

"I suppose you young gentlemen would like to go
ashore, wouldn't ye?"

"Yes, sir; oh! yes, sir,"
was the eager and unanimous response.

"Well, ye—a—ca-an't—go,"
the old cuss.drawled out, and stumped off into the
cabin.

WIND IT, JACK.

I never saw a sailor that claimed to have any stock
in babies, but they *tell* of one who came up to the
font to have his baby baptized, and, of course presented the infant, feet foremost.

"The other way,"
said the minister benignly, and Jack accordingly
turned the infant upside down.

"Excuse me," said the clergyman, "I mean the
other way."

So back came the embryo foretopman to the first
position again, to the evident discouragement of all
hands.

* "Wind it, Jack," said the nautical assistant, and,

---

*When a ship is swung half way round, or bow for stern, the opera-
tion is termed *winding* ship.

with an "Aye, aye, sir," Jack promptly turned the baby "end for end," and it was duly christened head first.

I started out to tell of the *great* earthquake, I believe, and I see that I have wound up with a little one. Well, perhaps, I may get to it in another letter.

LETTER XV.

Imprison'd fires, in the close dungeons pent,
Roar to get loose, and struggle for a vent;
Eating their way, and undermining all,
Till with a mighty burst whole mountains fall."

ON THE SOUTH PACIFIC STATION—THE EARTHQUAKE.

This is really about the earthquake this time, though I am well aware that it will not prove as interesting to you as it was to the Peruvians.

One beautiful afternoon in the year 1868—it don't make any material difference what time of year it was, as only an expert could tell the difference between summer and winter—the P. S. N. Co.'s steamer Santiago, bound south from Panama, came into the open harbor of Chala, Peru, and anchored; in an instant the custom-house officers were along side and on board, with several of the prominent merchants, all eager for the letters and news from the north, this line of steamers being their only channel of communication with the outside world, shut in as they were, by the lofty and almost impassable Andes mountains, whose snow-clad peaks towered above them, reaching an altitude of 20,000 feet, within thirty miles of the town.

Suddenly the confused babel of cries from the balsas, and innumerable small boats surrounding the steamer, united in a terrified shout of

"TERRE MOTO," "TERRE MOTO,

and away they pulled toward the shore. There were one or two North American ladies on board, who, leaning idly over the rail, were curiously watching the, to them, novel scene. They heard the shout and were startled by seeing the boats suddenly pull frantically toward the shore. What could "*terre moto*" mean; the passengers on board wrung their hands and threw themselves face downwards on the decks, moaning and crying as if they expected instant death. On shore a cloud of dust enveloped the town; the low *adobe* houses rocked, swayed and fell, the dry pulverized earth mounting in a cloud heavenward; the merchants from Chala, who had come on board, begged to be put on shore, but the captain refused to man a boat. Suddenly the sea rose,

"*El mar*,"

shrieked the frightened wretches, groveling on the decks in a very paroxysm of terror.

"*Nombre de Dios! El mar*."

The sea rose between the ship and shore, and swept, in a wave from forty to fifty feet in height, over the town, rising and falling with great rapidity, marking on the dry, sandy cliff the height of the water, far above the highest house; and the town, the pretty little Town of

CHALA WAS DESTROYED.

Back and forth sped the vessels lying, or which had been lying, at anchor; some went down; some were driven out to sea; some whirled round like tops, while the iron steamer trembled and rattled as if she were striking on the bottom of the bay.

One vessel quite near, that seemed to be in a whirlpool, she swung round so rapidly, had three persons on board, who rent the air with their cries; volunteers being called for, a boat was quickly manned from the Santiago, and the men, flinging themselves into the water, were rescued and brought on board.

By this time the water was so disturbed that the captain of the Santiago determined to seek safety farther off, and not a moment too soon; for just then the steamer tugged violently and parted her anchor chain, and away she went seaward, under full steam, and on top of a receding wave that left bare the spot where she had been anchored two minutes before in five fathoms of water.

It was a narrow escape, for if she had touched the bottom, the next wave would have swept over her, and the details of the earthquake, so far as the Santiago could furnish, would have been, like the town of Chala, lost.

There were some passengers on board for Chala, besides the merchants, who could not get ashore, and they were nearly distracted; but the captain would not yield, and kept on his course toward Arica, some 200 miles to the southward.

ARICA

was a very pretty little town about 400 miles southeast from Callao, and situated in the old bed of a river, with lofty mountains on each side; a railroad ran along near the sea, back round the mountain, some thirty miles to the town of Tacna. There was a mole, or wharf, a custom-house and a number of pretty houses, with a grove of olive trees, which maintained a bare existence, being watered carefully and tended as a curiosity almost, by the inhabitants of this otherwise dreary, dreary coast town. The United States steamer Wateree, a double-ender, and the store ship Fredonia, were stationed here; and, by-the-by, orders detaching me from the Tuscarora, and ordering me as executive officer of the Fredonia were on board that very steamer, the Santiago, so Arica promised to be a very interesting place to me, I assure you; and, too, there were passengers on board for Arica, who asked piteously of the captain if he really thought that the earthquake had reached as far south as Arica; others, who had left Callao in the steamer, were equally anxious about their homes, as they were speeding away from them; for they must go on; there was no stopping, and no place to stop.

Well, the steamer came in sight of the town about eight o'clock in the morning; there was the town, certainly, but where was the shipping; where was the Fredonia; where the custom-house; what had become of the olive grove and several large trees for which this little place was noted?

Halloo! there's the Wateree about 400 yards up on the beach. She seems to be all right, with her boats hoisted, her flag flying, but what is she doing so far from the water?

Soon a boat pulled off to the steamer and brought

THE NEWS OF THE EARTHQUAKE

in Arica. The town was destroyed; the Fredonia went down with all hands; the merchant ship Chañarçillo lay on the beach with her chain wrapped thrice around her, showing that she had been rolled over and over by the waves; that ship, there, on the beach with her back broken, is the Peruvian corvette America. The Wateree is up there, back of where was once the olive grove, all right and no one hurt, and so on with a long list of casualties.

"Have you any water to spare captain; the distilling works on the beach were destroyed, and we have no water. There is enough in the little stream to quench the thirst of the people left, but there is great suffering, notwithstanding."

The Santiago went on from port to port, listening to stories which were a mere repetition of what had gone before, until we struck Valparaiso, where a large number of vessels lay at anchor in the deep waters of the bay. Here they had had no earthquake, no tidal wave, beyond a trifling rise in the water, and were astonished to hear the story brought by the Santiago, of the ruins and desolation she had witnessed.

The Tuscarora was at once ordered to Arica with supplies for the suffering people, and we sailed in three or four days for that port.

On arriving at Arica I went on shore to see the ruin that had been caused by the earthquake. I can better describe the appearance if you can imagine the scene of some great conflagration,

LIKE CHICAGO AFTER THE FIRE,

without the mark of fire itself. The buildings had been crushed, and parts of them washed into the sea by the waves. The people had erected sheds, tents, and all sorts of contrivances to keep off the sun (there's no rain in Peru to keep off), and the destitution and suffering were very great. As we landed on the beach and started up toward the town two

nice-looking girls, black as the ace of spades, passed
us, and after the custom of the country said,

"*Buenas dias, caballeros.*"

"*Buenas dias, señoritas,*"
we gravely responded, raising our caps, and kept on
our way, half expecting to hear a "yah, yah," such
as we might have heard in our own country.

The English consul, an old resident of Arica,
described to me the fearful day substantially as follows :

"I felt the rocking of the house, and thought perhaps it was only a *temblor* (a word corresponding to
shake and not dangerous), but as it continued violently, I was convinced that it was an earthquake,
terre moto, and, calling my family to me, we gained
the street. The nurse, with my youngest child,
started for the mole, but I compelled her to come
back with me, and we turned to the mountain. Just
then, the earth opened beneath my feet and warm
water came up ankle deep, where before it was dry
sand. Sulphurous vapors filled the air, and what
with the dense clouds of dust caused by the falling
of houses, it was impossible to see in any direction,
and almost suffocating.

> "'With hue like that when some great painter dips
> His pencil in the gloom of earthquake and eclipse.'

"We gained, however, the principal street leading

up from the sea, and staggered along towards the mountains.

"THE GROUND SHOOK AND ROLLED

so that we reeled and staggered like drunken men. On either hand we saw people crushed beneath their houses, groaning piteously and calling on their saints to deliver them. Recognizing me they called out,

"'O, Señor Consul, ayudame por l'amor de Dios, y de todos los santos, salve me!'

"But I could not aid them; I had enough to help, and so passed on. Gaining that hill yonder, I turned and looked towards the sea. There were hundreds of people crowded on to the mole, when suddenly there was a cry of

"'El mar, El mar' (the sea, the sea),

and I saw the water recede, leaving the ground bare for a mile from the beach. The Fredonia store-ship had four anchors down, moored head and stern, and when the water went out it left her high and dry, heeled over to starboard. The Wateree went seawards at about twenty miles an hour, considerably faster than she ever went before, I guess, or will ever again. Several of the merchant ships got foul of each other, and everything on the water seemed endowed with life.

"As we stood there the sea returned in a wall of water, over forty feet in height, bringing the ships in with it.   The water struck the Fredonia and passed over her; on it came, and broke over the custom-house.   Again the sea receded, but the Fredonia had disappeared, crushed beneath that wall of water which had licked up all of that vast crowd on the mole.

"Again and again, until nine times, the sea came in and out, each time the wave a little smaller, until it finally ceased.   The America you see on the beach; the Chanarçillo as well, with her chain wrapped three times round her; the Wateree, too, 400 yards from high-water mark, is

THE ONLY VESSEL UNINJURED.

"The rest have all gone down.

"The wife of the executive officer of the Fredonia went down in her.   Lieut. J.'s wife is dead.   Her husband carried her in his arms to the hill, and found that she was dead, killed by the fall of the keystone of the arch of the house; the town, as you see, is destroyed; the people are starving; they cannot get away, as they have no money to pay their fare on the steamer, and there is no other way.

"The railroad track was torn up for miles; the heavy iron columns of the custom-house were twisted, broken and carried two miles from their original position; the old grave-yard, the other side of the bluff, was laid bare, and hundreds of corpses (mummies, Kilpatrick called them), exposed to view, curious old Indian pipes and relics being scattered about."

I went on board the Wateree and found her quietly resting at the foot of a hill, with her anchor down and a little astern of her, showing that at some period of her flight she had been farther in shore than where she now rested. Had she grounded then, on the hill, instead of at the foot of it, it is more than probable that she would have rolled down the hill and killed all hands on board. While on board, nearly every day the ship would shake from stem to stern, and the iron stack would rattle with the movement of the *temblor*, and we would run on deck to see the frightened people hurrying from their temporary homes in fear and dread of another *terre moto*.

We rode out one day on mule back to the English consul's new residence, some three miles from Arica. The road was over a hot, dusty, sandy incline, up the mountain, the crust sounding hollow under our animals' hoofs. The wife of the consul, a bright little woman, received us very cordially and gave us a glass of Pisco sherry.

She was much amused, when in answer to her question I said,

" *Mi muela* (back tooth) *no anda bien*," instead of *Mula* (mule).

On our return, as we rode along, smoking, a big negress stopped us with the salutation,

"*Deme un puro, caballeros*" (give me an Havana segar, gentlemen),

and walked off highly delighted, smoking a segar four inches long.

LETTER XVI.

"In sheets of rain the sky descends,
 And ocean swell'd with waters upward tends;
 One rising, falling one, the heavens and sea
 Meet at their confines in the middle way."

FROM CALLAO TO PANAMA IN 1869—THE TRADE-WINDS
AND THE COAST CURRENTS—A NIGHT ON DECK IN
THE BAY OF PANAMA—AN UNHERALDED STORM—
STEERING BY INFERENCE — PAST THE ROCKS IN
SAFETY—A CLEAR SKY AND A GOOD ANCHORAGE—
THE TIDES IN THE BAY OF PANAMA—THE RETURN
TO CALLAO—THE QUARTER-DECK—A BULLY STORY
—PAT MURPHY'S ROOSTER.

One warm day in June, 1869, the United States
ship Onward, to which I was attached, was ordered
to proceed from Callao, Peru, to Panama for stores
for the squadron. The Onward was a half clipper,
and sailed beautifully. We got under weigh, and

WITH EVERYTHING SET, ALOW AND ALOFT,

and with stun-sails both sides, we ran swiftly along
to the northward, borne on by the Peruvian current
and trade-wind toward Panama.

The trade-wind blows throughout the year, varying
from south to south southeast, freshening, at Callao,
with unvarying regularity, at 4 P. M. each day.

The Peruvian and Mexican coast currents correspond somewhat to the gulf stream of the Atlantic, flowing northward from Chili to Oregon, at the rate of about two knots per hour, tempering materially the climate of the countries past which they flow.

In about a week,

WE ENTERED THE BAY OF PANAMA,

at sunset, and hoped to reach our anchorage the same evening.

As we proceeded, however, the wind continuing to haul, we took in the studding-sails and braced the yards sharp up. It was now about two bells (9 P. M.), and being unable to weather the point we tacked and stood off shore.

The wind now almost died away, and we made only about three knots an hour, so I took the deck, and with the navigator, we tacked back and forth all night. We had a small crew, and had to work all hands all night, but as they lay down at their stations and slept until called up by the order "ready about," they did not suffer much. As for Charley C., the navigator, and myself, we drank brandy and water and smoked Havanas all night under a clear tropical sky, rousing the men up about every two hours to tack ship.

A PREMONITION.

At 8 o'clock A. M. the officer of the forenoon watch took the deck and I went down for some coffee; for some reason, however, I felt restless and uneasy, and soon came up on deck again, allowing the officer to go below. The sea was like glass; the ship had every sail set, to royal and flying jib, but lay motionless on the water, "as idle as a painted ship upon a painted ocean." Two or three miles away was Ship Rock, while beyond was the harbor of Panama, with its long lines of reefs, sharp as knives, as an unlucky vessel soon finds when she strikes one of them.

I looked around the horizon, but saw nothing unusual save a darkish cloud off the quarter. From habit I looked at the compass, and noted that the Columbian man-of-war Bolivar bore N. N. W. from us, about six miles distant.

SUDDENLY THERE WAS A RUSHING SOUND, and the storm was almost upon us.

"Top-gallant and royal clewlines! Flying jib down haul!" I shouted; "quick's your play."

"In royal and top-gallant sails; down flying jib!"

"Fore and main clew garnets and buntlines."

"Haul taut; up courses!

"Hands by the topsail halliards!"

"A hand in the chains."

11

The ship was now bounding along about twelve miles an hour; the rain fell in torrents, so that you could not *see* the bow of the ship; half an hour would bring us on the reefs; you could tell nothing from a chart, as we were in a land-locked harbor.

"Keep her N. N. W., quartermaster," I said, as I remembered the bearing of the Bolivar.

"N. N. W ?" asked the navigator, doubtingly, as he ran up the hatch.

"Are you sure ?"

"Yes," I said, "but you had better keep a sharp lookout for Ship Rock on the port bow, unless you want to swim for it."

"What water ?" I asked the man in the chains at the lead, who looked as if a cascade had exploded over him.

"Can't get bottom, sir; going too fast," he replied.

"It's somewhat important to know, Burns," I said, cheerfully, "and we're going faster than I really wish to myself."

"There she is," came from a score of eager throats, as Ship Rock loomed up majestically through the driving rain, on our port bow, and I knew that

WE WERE HEADED ALL RIGHT.

We could see by the change in the color that we were shoaling our water rapidly, so I clewed up the topsails and let her run on, driven only by the force of the wind on the sails, as they hung ready for furling.

> "A ship which hath struck sail doth run
> By force of that force which before it won."

After running for about ten minutes this way, the speed of the ship was so much reduced, that the leadsman got bottom, and called out:

"By the mark, five."

> "The lead once more the seaman flung,
> And to the watchful pilot sung
> 'Quarter less—five.'"

And I tell you we were glad to hear from him, too. Judging that we were about where we ought to be, and where we "would do the most good," we put down the helm, and as she came up head to the wind, and commenced to go astern, down went the starboard anchor. The rain stopped instantly,

THE SKY CLEARED AT ONCE,

the sun came out red-hot, and we were in as nice a berth as if we had taken all day to pick it out. But I don't want to do so any more. Talk about turning gray in a single night ! Some of us turned green in half an hour, and haven't quite recovered from it yet.

Well, about 4 o'clock, after furling sail and seeing all snug, the captain, who had been very sick in the cabin during the whole trip, and myself, took the gig and pulled ashore to Panama, distant about three and a half miles. The sun was very hot, but the men were in cool white, and, with the awning spread, pulled leisurely in to the landing.

A TREMENDOUS TIDE.

All of the large steamers and shipping are obliged to anchor about three and a half miles from Panama, out in the bay, on account of the tremendous rise and fall of the tide—twenty-five feet. At low tide you can walk out on the reefs a mile and a half from the wharf, where at high tide, there is fifteen feet of water. It is very frequent for captains to warp their vessels into a suitable place, shoring them up as the tide falls, until, left high and dry, such cleaning or repairs are made as can be done during the six hours of low water.

Panama is a *free* port, and we took occasion to lay in all sorts of stores, wines, cigars and liquors, which were very cheap indeed, there being no duty on them. We unwillingly laid in a few scorpions and centipedes also, which had concealed themselves in the old stores when at the store-house. They did not prove dangerous, however, as they lose their poison on board ship, where they have no poisonous thing to feed upon. In Panama, however, we always took the precaution to look into our slippers before putting them on in the morning to be sure that there were no centipedes in them.

OFF TO THE TURTLE ISLANDS.

After spending a few weeks at Panama, we got under weigh and stood out to sea to the westward, close hauled on the port tack.

The wind blew steadily from the south by west, and we ran along west by south for several hundred miles, passing close to the Gallapagos, or Turtle Islands, which lie just on the equator and west of Ecuador.

Large numbers of turtles are shipped from these islands to all parts of the world, as they are very cheap, and require no food, being stowed in the hold of the ship, without particular attention, for four or five months.

FIFTY-THREE DAYS CLOSE HAULED ON THE PORT TACK.

As we stood off shore, the wind veered gradually to the eastward, and when about 2,200 miles from the coast, we were running nearly due south. We ran on, still on the port tack, "full and by," until we sighted Easter Island, a lone island in the Pacific seldom visited by vessels.

Here we struck the trades, and ran in due east past the Island of Juan Fernandez toward Valparaiso, in 33 south latitude, and getting the wind dead aft came a-flying with studding-sails set both sides.

We arrived at Callao, which is in a straight line from Panama, distant 1,300 miles, in sixty-three days, having sailed 7,400 miles and having been close-hauled on the port tack fifty-three days.

THE QUARTER-DECK.

The quarter-deck of a man-of-war is the sacred place of the ship. No one crosses it without saluting by raising his cap; no one laughs, talks, or whistles on the quarter-deck; from the quarter-deck, are read all general orders, and the articles of war. Every Sunday divine service is read on the quarter-deck.

Whenever an officer, however high his rank, comes on deck, he salutes the *deck;* and the officer of the watch is required to invariably return the salute.

The starboard side of the quarter-deck, in port, or the weather side, at sea, is to be kept clear, and no one save the commander, the executive, and the officer of the watch, is permitted to use that side unless his duty compels it.

It is the one sacred spot on board ship that cannot be profaned with impunity.

SIZE OF SAILS.

I was asked the other day about how large was the largest sail on board the Sabine.

The length of the main-yard of the frigate Sabine, which was only a second rate, was 105 feet, and the drop of her mainsail 65 feet, taking 14,000 yards of canvas for an entire single suit of her sails. If her main-yard was laid on top of the Bank Block, Griswold street, Detroit, it would reach nearly over the Seitz Block and the foot of the sail would drag on the side walk.

EASE OFF YOUR SPANKER SHEET.

A sailor was coming across a meadow one day when a bull took after him, of course, he made for the fence; when almost there, he looked back over his shoulder, and seeing that the bull was close aboard, with his tail sticking straight out behind him, he shouted:

"Ease off your spanker sheet, and port your helm or you'll be afoul of me."

THAT INFERNAL OLD ROOSTER.

One dark night, about midnight, one of our blockading gunboats, off Mobile, commanded by a jolly commander, since in command of the Michigan on the lakes, was prowling around, seeking something to devour, when suddenly a cock was heard to crow to seaward.

In an instant, every man was on the alert, the quick-witted sailor knew that cocks didn't crow at sea, unless there was some vessel in that direction, to crow from, and they all knew, from their sharpened appetites, that it couldn't be from a blockader, as every old rooster in the squadron had been eaten up long ago. It was so dark that you could not see a ship's length away, so, carefully shrouding every light that could betray them, the steamer's head was turned in the direction of the friendly warning, and she stole quietly seaward.

In a very few minutes, the black hull of a vessel loomed up out of the darkness, and the boats being softly lowered, they took possession of the prize, a blockade runner, almost before the captured vessel was aware of it.

On going into the cabin of the prize, Capt. J. found that it was commanded by Pat Murphy, an old classmate of his, who had thought it his duty to ally his fortunes with those of his southern State.

"Look here, Jim," said Murphy, after a glass of wine had mellowed up matters a little, "how in the d——l did you know *I* was *here*, I couldn't see *you* at *all*."

Jim laughed and flapping his arms,

" Cock-a-doodle doo," said he.

"That infernal old rooster !" said Murphy, "I had given orders to cut his head off to-morrow."

"I am awful glad you put it off, Pat," said J., "here's to his health; he's worth ten thousand dollars to me."

LETTER XVII

"Oh, I am a cook and a captain bold,
And the mate of the Nancy brig,
And a bo'sun tight, and a midshipmite,
And the crew of the captain's gig."

SATURDAY AND ITS DELIGHTS—THE NAVAL OFFICERS
OF THREE NATIONS AT THE PRESIDENT'S BALL IN
SANTIAGO—THEIR SUCCESS AT MAKING THEMSELVES
UNDERSTOOD—HOW THEY SECURED PARTNERS, AND
HOW THEY ENJOYED THE DANCING—AN EVENING
ON BOARD SHIP—SAILOR BALLADS.

It was Saturday morning, and every one knows
what Saturday is on board a man-of-war. Thursday
we had scrubbed hammocks, and had dodged under
the dripping strips of canvas, stopped on the hammock gantline, in a rainbow fore and aft the ship,
from stem to stern. Friday morning the men had
scrubbed and washed clothes, and the results had
been dripping from the sea-lines between the main
and mizzen rigging for two hours, over the port side
of the quarter-deck, and now, Saturday, a general
cleaning day was upon us.

HOLY-STONES AND PRAYER-BOOKS.

The men were all busy getting up the heavy holy-
stones and sand, with the smaller ones, called prayer-

books, because the operators have to go on their
hands and knees with them to scour out the many
corners on board ship. "A hand from each part of
the ship" was on the catamaran,* armed with brooms,
brushes, sand and canvas, scrubbing copper; the
battery was cast loose and run in and out as required,
to enable the men to drag the heavy holy-stones back
and forth over the decks, where the guns had been.
The chain pumps were going; buckets of water
splashing all over the decks; quarter gunners scrubbing their sponge and rammer handles; quartermasters, with a pile of bridge gratings to holy-stone;
the officer of the deck, barefooted, with his breeches
rolled up to his knees, was pattering about, while the
executive officer, in similar attire, was making himself disagreeable by being everywhere, above and
below, pointing out new worlds to conquer, and seeing everything.

Well, as I was only the navigator and could not
scrub my sextants or wash out my chronometers very
well, I said smilingly to the envious and bedraggled
executive officer, my superior,

"I will go on shore, with your permission," and
accordingly I got on shore as soon as I could, and

---

* The term "catamaran" as used here means a small raft upon
which the sailor stands when scrubbing the copper on the exterior of
the ship.

returned in the afternoon, to find everything clean and neat, scrubbed inside and out, the guns secure, the running rigging flemished down, and the men sitting quietly about the decks with their ditty bags alongside, some one sewing on a blue shirt, another making a cap, while a third was busy on some intricate embroidery in various colors, representing, generally, a scarlet ship with blue guns and yellow masts, proudly careening under full sail, over a bright green sea, spotted here and there with a white cap.

Forward, on the gun-deck, the paymaster's steward, and his assistant, the Jack of the Dust, were serving out small stores, and one was drawing pots and pans, another soap and tobacco, while a slender little fellow was struggling with a No. 1 flannel shirt, or a pair of satinet trowsers a mile too big for him, recalling the frequent simile on board ship of,

"Oh, yes; it fits him like a purser's shirt on a handspike."

THEY CAN'T PUT YOU IN IRONS FOR THAT.

Away forward on the gun-deck, near the manger, and by the heel of the bowsprit, sits a sullen and discontented landsman. He is in the brig for punishment, with hands and feet in irons. A sympathetic shipmate, on the port side, finds time, when the sentry is not looking, to ask:

"What are you in for, Bill?"

"Why, only for spitting on deck and sassing the captain of the top,"
is the answer of the aggrieved aspirant for naval honors.

"Pshaw! they can't put you in irons for that," said the sympathizer.

"Oh, they *can't*, eh?" witheringly replied the pris-- oner; "well, what in thunder am I doing here?"

A PROTEST.

Apropos of the above, the late Capt. S—— used to tell a story himself, illustrating the power of the commanding officer in the old time to do pretty much as he pleased whether right or wrong. He was a lieutenant on board the old North Carolina, and was somewhat startled one day by an order sent from the cabin for Lieut. S—— to take the launch and go to Sandy Hook for sand. Up he jumped and storming on deck, sent in his name, by the orderly, to see the captain.

"Good morning, Mr. S——," said the old skipper.

"Ahem! Good morning, captain. I just received an order from you to go for sand, sir, and thinking that there was some mistake, I came up to ask—ah."

"There's no mistake, Mr. S——. You are to take the launch and go for sand."

"But, sir, I am a lieutenant, sir. It has always been the duty of a midshipman or a past-midshipman, sir, to go for sand."

"You will take the launch, sir, and go for sand," coldly replied the master of the situation.

"But, captain—a—a—I—a—*protest*, sir !"

"You may protest, and be—a—as much as you like, Mr. S——, but in the mean time go for sand."

And he went.

AN EVENING ON BOARD SHIP.

The evening, on board ship in port, is much enjoyed by all hands. The officers smoke and gossip on the port side of the quarter-deck, the commander on the poop, and the men in little circles forward. Some play at dominos by the light of the moon, or near one of the fixed lights of the ship; others spin yarns, about "when they were in the old States frigate," or, "I was a coming round the Horn once, in '47, I think," or, "did I ever tell you about me and Capt. Wilkes, when we was on a exploring expedition to the South Pole?" etc.; but there is always sure to be a fair audience gathered round some good singer, who tips 'em a shanty in good old sepulchral baritone, the audience coming in *strong* on the chorus.

That night upon the larboard
   Ben Backstay's ghost appeared,
And from his open lips
   These awful words were heered;
   These awful words were heered.

" With a chip chow,
   Cherry chow, fol de rol de diddle;
And a chip chow,
   Cherry chow, fol de rol de day.

" ' Now shipmates all assembled,
   Take warning by my fate,
And when you take your liquor down
   Be sure and take it straight;
   Be sure and take it straight.'

" With a chip chow," etc.

Another heart-rending ballad was in eighty-four verses, and was entitled,

"THE LOSS OF THE OLD PEACOCK.

" In '48 we left Old Point
   T'explore for a southern land,
Our ship ataut from keel to truck,
   And with proud seamen manned.
We hove our anchor short apeak
   At the dawning of the day,
And by six bells in the morning watch
   Were fairly under way.

CHORUS—(*strong*).

" Shan de loo ral loo ral li do,
   Shan de loo ral lay.
Shan de loo ral loo ral li do,
   Shan de loo ral *la—a—a—y*," etc.

At 8.45 the drum and fife begin and play various tunes, until 9 P. M., when the officer gives the order, " Roll off."

At the third roll, the bell strikes two, the whistles "pipe down," and all hands turn in.

As soon as the whistles cease, the two cornets play a duet—"Home, Sweet Home," or some pretty old ballad, which sounds inexpressibly beautiful coming over the water on a calm summer night. Later the officers seek their rooms, and all is quiet, save the tramp of the restless watchers to and fro.

THE PRESIDENT'S BALL.

> "A man in all the world's new fashion plante!,
> That hath a mint of phrases in his braid."

The President of the Republic of Chili had sent an urgent invitation for all the naval officers of the ships of the various nationalities lying in the bay of Valparaiso, to come to the president's ball at Santiago, the capital, adding that transportation had been furnished and a special train would convey us to Santiago, 150 miles distant. Accordingly, about a dozen of us, French, English and American, presented ourselves, *en grande tenue*, cocked hat, sword, epaulette and swallow tail, at the ball-room. Strange as it may appear, the Englishman who had been two years on the coast, and "could never pick up the lingo you know," spoke English; the three Frenchmen spoke good French, although there was one of them that looked so like an American that I was constantly bewildering him, by bantering him in English, of which he understood not one word, to speak English.

Now, I would say,

" Why don't you talk. You're a Yankee, you know you are, and can talk just as well as I can; that's too thin, you are no Frenchman,"
and he would smile and show his white teeth, and shrug his shoulders, not having a glimmering, even, of what I said. The Americans spoke pure American, with occasional dashes of French, not always *apropos*, but good in their way, and helping to disguise their meaning better than their English would. Well, we loafed around the magnificent ball-room a few times, admiring from afar the many richly dressed brunettes, hoping that we might be introduced to them. The band was playing the most delightful waltz, and the chorus of ladies, singing with the orchestra, was simply magnificent (these Chilenas are very fine musicians), and we knew that *we* could waltz readily in any language.

Well, as I remarked,

WE LOUNGED ROUND THE HALL,

dragging our swords and holding our cocked hats on our arms, comparing notes on each round, and adjourning to the supper room at intervals, where an elegant supper was spread and champagne flowed freely, until I thought I should have dropped. The Englishmen looked red and mad, the Frenchmen indifferent, and the Americans disgusted. I went up to a fellow in "sojer" clothes, that I took to be one of the committee, and conversed with him on the subject animatedly in French, English, American and Spanish, uniting them all impartially in the same sentence, and emphasizing the whole with gestures in all the living and dead tongues, the little band of mariners from Valparaiso anxiously watching the result. I finished a somewhat incoherent appeal as follows:

"Look here, Señor, *ne pourez vous pas*, present me to some of these señoritas to dansez, you know. *Je suis* American naval officer, and I don't *connais* any of the people, *et je desire* to dance, and so do the other fellows."

Here the other fellows nodded vigorously and said: "*Si, si.*"

Well, the committeeman said *suivez moi*, and I told the other fellows he says *suivez moi*, and if he introduces me to any of 'em I'll fix you fellows all right.

I think

I FOLLOWED THAT VILLAIN

about an hour, round and round the hall; every now and then I would pull his sleeve and say,

"Señor, there's a nice-looking girl, introduce me to her," and he would reply,

" *Esperé un poco,*"

which, in the language of the modern Castilian
means, hope a little, or, more freely translated, hold
on.   As we wearily traversed the immense hall, I
would encounter now and then my American Frenchman, and would accost him with,

" *Est ce que vous avez dansé encore mon garçon ?* "

"*Pas encore,*"

he would cheerfully reply, and go out and take a
drink, while I was obliged to follow my leader and
couldn't go with him.

Just then I caught sight of Charley C——, madly
galloping around with a little girl, and I angrily
deserted my guide and rejoined my friends.   One of
our officers had found a little English boy, he said,
and he was carrying on quite a conversation with
him; at least, he thought he was, but I ascertained
that the little English boy spoke nothing but Spanish.

Well, we went home, to the hotel, about 3 A. M.,
none of us having danced at all except Charley C——,
who had one gallop, and who informed us confidentially that he thought it wasn't likely that he should
ever get her to dance another with him.   After
spending the next day in Santiago, we started down
to the depot to take the train for Valparaiso.

SOME SAILOR SPANISH.

I walked up to the ticket office, and throwing down a twenty-dollar gold piece asked for four tickets; the clerk pushed back the coin, with some remark in Spanish, and I endeavored to explain to him all about it, you know.

In vain I said this is American gold, and is worth twenty-one dollars and sixty cents, Chileno money: he pushed it back, saying,

"*No entiendo Ingles, Señor, y no se oro Americano,*"

so the paymaster pushed me one side, saying,

"Let me tell him."

Fixing his eagle eye firmly on the little Dago, he commenced:

"Look here, Señor, *nous sommes officiales Americana,* and we've come up to the president's ball, you know. *El bullo del Presidente,* you see; and *este oro, vale mas que el otro ;* do you sabe?"

The Chileno smiled blandly upon the enthusiastic linguist, and for the twenty-third time repeated calmly:

"*No entiendo Ingles, Señor !*" (I don't understand English, sir.)

"Now, get out of the way you fellows," said Charley, "and let *me* tell him."

Charley had made a cruise in the Mediterranean, and could speak *any* language.·

Planting himself squarely before the small window, he brought his port eye to bear on the placid countenance of the undisturbed official and said sternly,

" *Habla Español?* "

" *Si,*" promptly answered the Chileno.

" *Parlez vous Français, bueno?* " somewhat incoherently pursued Charley, following up his advantage.

" *Mira, Señor,*" and thinking that *Mira* sounded well he said it again.

" *Nosotros sommes Americanus et* we come up to the president's ball, and that *oro* is worth more than your old Dago money by a dollar and sixty cents, and if you don't choose to take that money we'll ride down in your derned old wagon for nothing."

" *No entiendo Ingles,*" replied the imperturbable clerk, and our stock of language was exhausted.

Fortunately a gentleman, better posted in the value of American gold, gave us four Chileno five-dollar pieces for a twenty, and we rode down to Valparaiso in triumph.

LETTER XVIII.

"Some pick out bullets from the vessel's side,
Some drive old oakum through each seam and rift."

CAPTURING A DESERTER ON BOARD A PERUVIAN MAN-
OF-WAR — THE LINGUISTIC DIFFICULTIES OF THE
PERUVIAN NAVY—BILLY'S $800 TEMPERANCE LEC-
TURE — FOREIGN NOBLEMEN AS CADETS AT THE
UNITED STATES NAVAL ACADEMY — AS COOL AS
"MIDSHIPMAN EASY"—WHAT A SECRETARY OF THE
NAVY KNEW ABOUT SLOOPS.

You remember reading a short time ago, an account
of the engagement of two or three English men-of-
war with the Peruvian iron-clad Huascar, in which
the latter vessel appeared to considerable advantage.

AFTER A DESERTER.

I went on board the Huascar some years ago, while
attached to a ship in the harbor of Callao, to look for
a deserter. The officer of the deck, a trim little
Peruvian, with a very small waist, and very pegtop
trousers, received me very cordially and seemed eager
to oblige me in finding my man.

"Von Schmidt?" he repeated after me.

"*No le conozco*" (I don't know him).

I insinuated that he probably called himself now

Lopez de Vega, or Antonio Martinez Santo Campo instead of John Smith. Struck with the idea, he turned to the boatswain's mate, an old English man-of-war's man apparently, and addressing him in Spanish, as Patron, he volubly gave directions that Antonio Garçia be sent to the mast. The old fellow stared at him, and then walked across the deck to a *genuine* Dago, and asked in an under-tone,

" What in thunder did he say ? "

The answer must have been intelligible, for I soon heard his pipe and the cry,

" Anto-onio Garcy, do you hear there Garcy, you're wanted aft."

I laughed heartily at the idea of trying to run an American man-of-war, where the officers of the deck, and the boatswain's mate, spoke an entirely different language; it seemed to work well, however, for Garcy turned out to be plain Smith, and I bore him off in triumph.

RUNNING A SHIP IN SEVERAL LANGUAGES.

On another occasion the Independencia got under weigh and passed out near us. The anchor was up to the hawse-hole, and the officer of the deck, wishing to know if the cat-fall was hooked (I don't know what they call it in Spanish), called out,

" *Esta usted listo, Señor ?* " (Are you ready, sir ?) Back came the answer, in pure Anglo-Saxon,

"All ready with the cat, sir,"
and our amusement was at a climax, when the man
in the chains, heaving the lead, chanted out,

"And a quar-r-ter five-e."

The Peruvians are poor sailors, and not original, so
they employ English, American and German experts,
for continual examples to their mixed and otherwise
useless crews.

GOOD FRIDAY AT CALLAO.

One day in the harbor—I suppose it must have been
Good Friday—there was considerable of a commotion
in the squadron of French and Peruvian men-of-war
lying near us. At 12 o'clock noon the yards were
cockbilled, and the braces slackened up, making the
ships look as untidy and desolate as possible, and at
the first gun, out went an effigy at the fore yard-arm
of the flag-ship, swinging back and forth with the send
it got from the ship's side.

I was puzzled to know the meaning of the perform-
ance, until one of the quartermasters volunteered the
remark that "he guessed they were hanging Judas
Iscariot." And so it proved, and old Judas hung
there until sunset, when down he came, with the
colors, and the yards being squared and gear hauled
taut, the ships resumed their ordinary trim appearance.

BUYING A DIAMOND.

One of our gun-boats visited Rio on her way out to
join the Pacific squadron, and lay there for several
days.   One day one of the officers, a classmate of
mine, happened on shore, and having been at sea a
good while, took a drink or two to make up for lost
time.   As he walked down the street, opposite a large
jewelry store, he was hailed by the paymaster and
doctor to come over and buy or look at some diamonds.   Billy muttered something about not wanting
any diamonds just then, but good-naturedly joined
them.   They selected two modest diamonds, had
them marked and called to Billy to know how he
liked them.   He looked contemptuously at the little
brilliants, and majestically called on the merchant for
some *diamonds*.   None of your little trash, but some
of your big diamonds, and had marked for him a gem
as big as a three-cent piece.

The next day one of the officers said:

" Billy, when are you going ashore after your diamond ? "

" My what ? "

" Why the diamond you bought yesterday.   Don't
you know that you bought a diamond yesterday as
big as a dead-light, and had it marked for you ? "

Well, Billy interviewed the paymaster, drew,
begged and borrowed all the money he could, and

with a bag full of English sovereigns wended his way to a broker's office. Fortunately for him English gold was at a high premium, and on account of the Paraguayan war, milreis were at a discount, so he made the exchange, bought the diamond for about $800 in gold, and with a sorrowful heart came on board again, knowing that circumstances over which he had no control, would materially interfere with his going on shore any more for the next four months.

He sent the diamond home, however, and about a year after sold it for some $1,500. Notwithstanding, he says it was the most powerful temperance lecture he ever experienced.

NO REVERENCE FOR DUCAL RANK.

For the last ten or twelve years, there have been several foreign youths at the U. S. Naval Academy, being educated in all the branches taught there.

There are now several Japanese cadets there, and some twelve years ago the Duc de Penthievre, son of the Prince de Joinville, graduated from the Academy. It is very creditable to our young country that the children of the old should be sent to us for instruction and training, and the result has been so good that it is probable that our schools will always have some such representative under instruction.

The Duc was called Pierre d'Orleans at the Academy, and the midshipmen, with the true American reverence for rank, called him "Pete."

He was smart, quick, and a general favorite, and you may suppose that he could not have talked much of the blue blood of the Bourbons, and his long line of ancestry, and be popular.

He went out as navigator of one of the school ships on their summer cruise, and, one day was bothering a lieutenant who was sitting writing in his stateroom, by asking questions, pulling his hair, or something of the kind, until the lieutenant turned round and said deferentially,

"Oh, go away, King! Feet (he has tremendous feet), take his Royal Highness away. Look here, Penthy, if you don't get out of this I'll put a bigger head on you than you have got now."

The Duc rose to the rank of lieutenant, I think, then resigned, and, if I am not mistaken, was made admiral of the Brazilian navy.

I have heard frequently of the lavish hospitality he invariably shows to his old classmates whenever he encounters them.

C. WANTS TO GO TOO.

A number of years ago a couple of midshipmen were sitting in the steerage of one of our sloops-of-war; one, meditating with his heels against the door of his locker, the other, concocting a formidable letter to the Secretary of the Navy.

"What are you writing, Jimmy?" said the first.

"Writing for leave of absence for two weeks," was the reply.

"Tell 'em that I want to go, too, will you?"

"All right," said Midshipman Easy, quietly adding a P. S.:

"C. says that he wants to go too."

In a few days back came a letter from the Department for the enterprising midshipman, formally granting him two weeks' leave of absence agreeably to his request of the 15th instant, and adding,

"If midshipman C. desires leave of absence, the Department will be pleased to grant it, if he will make the application in proper form."

The midshipman has ever since been known by the sobriquet of "C. who wants to go too."

SLOOPS AND OAKUM.

A number of years ago, the then Secretary of the Navy was induced by the Advisory Board of Naval Officers to ask Congress for authority to build six sloops-of-war. The Secretary, a very able lawyer. but more conversant with the single-masted North River sloops than with men-of-war in general, was very much astonished when the first of the six sloops-of-war was put in commission.

Upon seeing a full-rigged, three-masted ship, costing some $750,000, instead of the sloop his imagination had pictured, he turned indignantly to the officers in attendance and said:

" Gentlemen, you have deceived me, these are not *sloops*, these are *ships*."

There is another, a rumor only, that a high official, on being told that oakum (old rope pulled apart for calking seams) was very scarce, said innocently:

" Why, didn't they plant as much as usual last year?"

LETTER XIX.

BULL-FIGHT AT LIMA, PERU — WHAT A BULL-RING IS
LIKE—THE BULL MAKES THE ATTACK—THE MATA-
DOR AND HIS SWORD—BULL NO. 1 DIES GAME—A
PLUCKY LITTLE BULL MAKES MATTERS LIVELY —
"THE KING OF THE PROTESTANTS"—TRUTHS
DOUBTED AND MUNCHAUSENISMS BELIEVED.

The Peruvian Fourth of July comes on the 28th,
I believe, and I went up to Lima on that day to see
a bull-fight.

THE BULL-RING

was circular, about 500 feet in diameter, having a
curved row of seats of eight or ten tiers, like a circus,
extending round the outer rim, a portion being divided
off into private boxes. I was fortunate enough to be
invited to accompany a party of young and old ladies,
and we had a box. There was seating capacity for
about 10,000 people, I should say, with many standing up. A fine band played between the acts, and
the scene was a very exciting one.

Shortly after we took our seats the gates opened
and some half a dozen horsemen, *caballeros*, rode into
the inclosure and round the ring. The horses were
very indifferent-looking ones, but proved to be quick

enough to keep out of the way. A large number, say fifteen *capadores*, were moving about the ring clad in fancy Spanish dress, doublet and hose, with scarlet-lined cloaks or capes.

Suddenly, amid a flourish of trumpets, the cattle gate opened and

IN BOUNDED A BULL

with long sharp horns. He seemed startled and some-what frightened at first, but, recovering himself, he started after a horseman, who had backed his horse into position, and furiously chased him round the ring. The horse seemed to canter or leap with the bull, so that though his horn was almost against the flank of the horse, he couldn't quite reach him.

Soon the *capadores* came round, and flaunting their gayly colored capes drew off the bull's attention by cries of

" *Toro! ah, Toro! mal Toro!* "

He would stand still and hesitate, and finally charge the nearest one, for, say fifty feet, when another would draw him off, and so on until he was almost exhausted. All this time they were firing off sky-rockets and fire-works, although it was broad day-light. Now my attention was called to a couple of gayly dressed men carrying rods called

BANDERILLOS,

with barbed-pointed ends, the rods being dressed
with cut paper. One of these, holding a dart in each
hand, followed the bull, taunting him to turn on him.
Suddenly the bull turned short round and charged
him; just as it seemed as if the lowered horns would
catch him, he quickly planted both *banderillos* into
the neck of the bull and darted to one side; the cut
papers strung out twenty feet in length ; the bull
pawed and tried to shake out the darts, but the hooks
stuck securely, and held them for a long time. Sometimes the darts have explosives in them, and burst
after a while, driving the poor animal almost mad.
And now the other *banderillero* plants his two darts
successfully in the bull's neck and he is almost beside
himself. By this time

THE CHEERFUL AUDIENCE HAS GROWN BLOODTHIRSTY,

and a cry goes up,
" *El Matador, El Matador !* " (the slayer),
and a fine-looking fellow sprang forward, carrying a
stout sword, about six feet in length, and a small red
cape. He approached the bull, and after several
attempts, induced the maddened animal to attack
him, as he had done the *banderilleros.* Finally, just
as the lowered head was close under his hand, he
struck his sword back of the fore shoulder almost to
the hilt, amid the cheers of the assembly.

THE POOR BULL STAGGERED,

vomiting blood—a few steps and fell, when a man ran quickly up and with a dagger severed the spinal cord at the neck, and bull No. 1 was dead.

While the *matador* advanced to the box of the *Municipalidad* (the common council), to receive a roll of silver soles (dollars), a team of six mules dashed in gayly caparisoned; the head of the bull was lifted on a low, two-wheel truck, chained, and, amid a burst of quick music from the band, away they dashed, making a circuit of the ring at a gallop, and dragged the bull from the ring. I should have said that the next bull had been standing in a small, close pen, with a kindly dago overhead, whose business it was to keep pricking him with a lance, to have him in trim when wanted.

Again the band played, again the gates opened, and

IN DASHED A SECOND BULL,

his gay blanket, not strapped on, but pinned to the hide at the four corners with fish-hooks so it wouldn't come off; he rushed swiftly to the center of the bull-ring, where a figure of a man turning a lathe run by fire-works was in operation; catching the figure on his horns he threw it high in the air as it exploded, and then trampled it under his feet amid a cloud of dust and burning powder.

The *capadores* approached him carefully, but he would not attack them beyond making a short run of a few steps; the audience murmured,

"*Mal toro no sirve, no vale nada,*"

and the *capadores* renewed their efforts, one catching the bull by the tail, but in vain; he wouldn't fight, and several other bulls being let in, the herd was driven ignominiously out by one man with a whip.

ONCE MORE A BURST OF MUSIC,

and another bull, a little fellow, came bounding in: he was as quick as lightning, and I tell you the *capadores* scattered; he possessed the disagreeable quality of sticking to one man at a time, in spite of the efforts of the others to draw him off. One fellow, closely pursued, could not reach one of the slips, and sprang up the wall of the ring, clambering into one of the boxes,

WITH THE BULL'S LONG SHARP HORN

just missing him by about an inch. As for me, I hoped that the bull would catch him; my sympathies were entirely with the bull. A *capadore* ran up on one side, and the bull started for him, and he had just time to reach one of the little barricades built up at intervals round the edge of the ring, with just room for a man to pass behind. Here he supposed himself safe, but the little bull followed him in, and

13

stuck when about one-third of the way in, the man
rolling out at the other side scared half to death.

"*Buen toro!*"

the people shouted and laughed, but only for a few
minutes. "Kill him," was soon the cry, and the
plucky little bull was murdered, as were his prede-
cessors.

SIX BULLS WERE KILLED

in two hours, and then a man came in on the bull's
back, having a strap round the body of the bull to
hold on to. He rode the animal round where the bull
chose to go, and, watching his opportunity, slid
off and escaped up the box fronts. For this feat the
bull became his property, and was driven out alive.

I noticed that the name of one of the young ladies
in our box was

AGRIPPINA,

and I remarked to her mother that it was a Bible
name.

"*Bible, que es eso?*"   (What is that?)

I said, "the Bible is our holy book."

"Oh! and she is in that, eh?"

"Yes, I am a Protestant. You know Agrippa
was king of the a—a— (what in thunder is Jews?
John, do you know what Jews is in Spanish?) King
of the a—a—"

"*De los Protestantes ?*" (Of the Protestants) said the old lady, anxious to help me out.

"*Esto es muy curioso ; mira, Agrippina, su nombre es la misma del Rey de los Protestantes.*" (That is very curious; look, Agrippina, your name is the same as the king of the Protestants.)

Fortunately the bull at this moment almost succeeded in ripping up a horse and rider, and the attention of the dear girls was attracted to the ring.

GEOGRAPHICAL AND CLIMATOLOGICAL INFORMATION.

One girl finally asked me:

"You live in New York ?"

"No, about 800 miles west of New York."

"Are there cities so far from New York ?"

"Oh, yes! I live near a lake of fresh water bigger than the whole state of Peru."

"Fresh water! Oh, Señor! there is no such thing ; and is the health good there ?"

"Good! why they had to kill a man out there the other day to start a grave-yard."

"*Nombre de Dios! Mira, Agrippina, necessitaba matar a un hombre para principiar un lugar de enterremiento.*" (Look, Agrippina! they had to kill a man to commence a place of interment.)

When I told them of the vast prairies covered with grass, of the groves of trees, of the thunderstorms, of the rain, and of the flashes of lightning, they looked at me with surprise that I should expect them to believe such nonsense. They never saw green things grow without patient watering and attention, and as for rain, why should they believe it ? they never had seen it rain in Peru.

LETTER XX.

"With roomy decks, her guns of mighty strength,
Deep is her draught, and warlike is her length."

A MIDSHIPMAN'S EXPERIENCE ON BOARD THE BRIG
PERRY—CHASE AND CAPTURE OF THE PRIVATEER
SAVANNAH—A CHOICE OF LIQUORS.

After graduating from the Naval Academy, I was
ordered in June, 1861, for duty on board

THE BRIG PERRY,

then fitting out from the New York Navy Yard.

Being a midshipman I was only entitled to quarters
in the steerage, but the partition having been pulled
down, I was perforce in the ward-room, swinging in
a hammock from whence I was turned out at six bells
(7 A. M.), to make room to set the ward-room breakfast table. The other officers slept in bunks around
the ward-room, with lockers for their clothes in front
or inboard of them, and these lockers furnished a
permanent seat for them at the mess table. The
captain had a small trunk cabin, a little higher and
abaft ours, to which entrance was gained from the
quarter-deck by a flight of three steps down. You
could not swing a kitten by the tail in either cabin
or ward-room, but possibly they didn't want any kit-

tens slung, and we got used to the small quarters after a while.

At the time, I thought the cabin magnificent, and two years afterward, when I might have had command of the Perry, I sneered contemptuously at the small quarters as they then appeared.

The lieutenant commanding the Perry died a few years ago a rear admiral; the executive officer, also a lieutenant, is now a commodore, the navigator a commander, and I, well, a historian.

ASTONISHING A CAPTAIN.

' There was always more or less feeling shown by the older officers against graduates of the Naval Academy, and the commanding officer took it for granted that I did not know much of anything, so for the first two weeks I did nothing but drill the men at small arms, then single sticks, and exercise my navigation with the navigator, taking sights and working the position of the ship.

From time to time I astonished the captain by exhibiting a knowledge of different subjects connected with the service, provoking the somewhat satirical question:

" Why, do they teach you *that* at the Naval Academy ? "

I remember on one occasion that he was really astonished because I worked out the position of the ship one day, and reported it to him, the navigator being sick, and how pleased he was, because the position, as found by the navigator at 4 P. M. of the same day differed from mine some thirty miles, and he attributed the error to me, and was correspondingly disgusted when the navigator generously claimed the mistake as his own.

NAVIGATION.

" Rude as their ships was navigation then,
   No useful compass or meridian known:
Coasting, they kept the land within their ken,
   And knew no north but when the pole-star shone."

By navigation on board a man-of-war, is meant not the conduct of the ship as regards the working of the ship itself, its evolutions and internal discipline, but simply the ascertaining correctly the exact position of the ship *at any* time upon the chart or map.

The latitude is ascertained usually by observations of the sun at high noon, though it may be obtained by observation of the moon and stars.

If the north star was exactly at the North Pole, instead of revolving a degree and a half from it, you could find the latitude simply by measuring its altitude, or height above the horizon; indeed, if you can see the north star, you can form a pretty tolerable guess how many degrees high it is, and such number of degrees will be about the latitude.

As a degree is sixty miles, you can readily see that
it will not do to guess at it if the safety of a valuable ship, freighted with valuable lives, depends upon
your accuracy. Knowing the latitude, we can find
the longitude by an observation of the sun, moon or
stars, if we are provided with a clock or chronometer
showing Greenwich time.

At the risk of being tedious, I will explain a little
the principle of

A TIME SIGHT.

The object is to find the time of day to a second.
If we know that, we compare it with our Greenwich
time, and the difference is our longitude. If our
time is five hours earlier than the Greenwich clock
shows, of course, we are five hours west of Greenwich, or five-twenty-fourths of 360 degrees, which is
75 degrees west longitude. In order to find the local
time, the navigator goes on deck at seven bells (7.30
A. M.), the sun being about twenty-five degrees high,
and with his sextant measures the height of the sun,
noting the time by watch or chronometer; having
the latitude, sun's altitude and the declination (which
latter is given for every day in the year in the
Nautical Almanac), he has three sides of a spherical
triangle to find one angle, which is the local apparent
time.

As an error of four seconds of time is equivalent

to one mile, it is of importance that this computation should be accurate. Of course, there are numerous corrections to be applied in the actual computation, such as dip, refraction, semi-diameter and parallax. Having found, therefore, the latitude and longitude, their intersection on the chart will be the position of the ship.

Well, we got under weigh one morning and sailed out to sea in the little brig, bound for the blockade off Charleston, South Carolina.

As it happened, the treasury of the United States was quite empty, and we could get no money, consequently the ward-room mess were unable to lay in any stores, and we lived on our rations of pork, beans, salt horse, etc. *Hot!* it was *red* hot, cooped up in that little box, a hundred and fifty of us; the water, too, was warm. The tanks were so small and the ship so small that she rode light, with little draft of water, and that of the warmest, I assure you.

CAPTURE OF THE SAVANNAH.

Well, we were detailed for the blockade of St. Mary's River, off Fernandina, Florida, to see that none of 'em got away, I suppose, and we perspired off that port for some weeks.

One day, when cruising between Charleston and Fernandina, I have forgotten whether going to or returning from Fernandina, we sighted two sail, a brig and a schooner, *suspicious, very* suspicious; so we went for them. The brig kept away to the eastward, while the schooner hauled her wind for the south. Following some occult train of reasoning of his own, our skipper concluded to follow the schooner; so we followed, keeping the chase to leeward of us on our port bow.

We followed out the rules for chasing to leeward, windward, etc., keeping him exactly on the same bearing and gaining on him.

We chased him from 4 P. M. until night, which was, fortunately for us, clear and bright, when our sails being dampened by the dew, and being more lofty than the schooner's, drew better, and we rapidly overhauled him.

About 9 P. M. we luffed up a little and sent a shot across his bows, which he returned with a shot, evidently aimed at the southern cross, for it went over the royal yard. As we lost way by luffing to bring our guns to bear, we concluded not to luff, but kept steadily on after him. By this time we had all got excited, and watched the flying schooner with great interest, taking frequent bearings to see if he had drawn ahead or fallen off. About 10.30 P. M. we had got so near that we braced up a little and brought our three guns and a howitzer on a side to bear, and we blazed away, the schooner returning some half a dozen shots.

By some extraordinary conduct I had so far won the confidence of the commander as to be intrusted with the sole control of one twelve-pound howitzer and four men, and I shot off that howitzer at the little schooner till I couldn't rest; a Gatling gun wasn't a patching to it. I suppose that schooner surrendered over a dozen times, but we were excited and fired away until, during a lull, the captain of the schooner, executing a war-dance on the deck of his little ship, shouted so loudly,

"I surrender. I surrender; don't shoot any more!" that we reluctantly ceased firing and sent a boat to him in charge of the second lieutenant.

In about half an hour the boat returned, having left a prize crew on board, and bringing the news that the prize was the privateer Savannah from Charleston, South Carolina, Baker commanding.

When the boat came alongside, a strange figure, in his shirt sleeves, came on board with Capt. Baker, remarking volubly and energetically:

"You've treated me all right aboard your old Stars and Bars, but if you'll excuse me, gentlemen, I am glad to get back to the old Stars and Stripes."

HE WAS DRUNK, YES, VERY DRUNK.

It transpired that the brig we saw had just been captured and a prize crew put on board, the Savannah taking the captain of the brig out before sending her away, and this was the captain.   He said, afterwards, that he did not usually drink, but was so blue over the loss of his ship that he got drunk to drown his sorrows.

The next morning they cleaned the schooner out, and threw over about fifty empty bottles—more rum than they had powder.

Capt. Baker said that he was just twenty-four hours out from Charleston; that this was the first privateer commissioned; that he had returned our fire until his pivot and only gun had kicked over the carriage, and then he surrendered.

One shot went through his foresail, one under the main boom, one carried away the jib, and his crew refused to do anything, but went below and got drunk.   So he lowered the sails himself and hollered " I surrender ! " until he was hoarse.

We sent the Savannah home to New York, and some ten years after I got about $50 prize money as my share of the capture.

We had a report on board ship that the merchants of New York, had offered a bonus of $60,000 for the capture of the first privateer of the war, and there

wasn't a man or boy on board that didn't figure
before night what his percentage of $60,000 would
be. We searched around for three or four days, but
we didn't catch the brig, and long afterward we
learned that she got safely into Georgetown.

GOBBLING A TUG.

Among the papers of the Savannah we found an
arrangement with the Charleston authorities that a
signal of three green lights and one red light preceded, and followed by a rocket, would mean that
the privateer Savannah was off the bar with a prize,
send a tug. So after consulting with the admiral our
wily commander determined to sneak close up to the
bar at midnight and entice a tug out and gobble it.

We secured the flagship's pilot, therefore, and
after lying all day, with our prize in plain sight of
the rebels, we got under weigh at dark and, in charge
of the pilot, we sailed softly in; every sailor was on
deck armed to the teeth, and midst great excitement,
all the greater because suppressed, we sailed, as I
remarked before, softly in. When we had reached a
spot which the pilot said, in a whisper, was the bar,
we took in the royal and top-gallant sails, hauled up
the courses, and braced the main-yard aback. With
the utmost secrecy a rocket was mysteriously brought
on deck and sent up, then, the quartermaster, who

had had his three green and one red light ready for the last hour, hidden in a division tub, trotted them out and hoisted them to the main truck. Another rocket was sent up and then we waited for the tug to come out and be gobbled. An hour passed, but no tug came.

Of course there must be some mistake. So the commander consulted the signal card again, but it was all right; so up went another rocket, the lanterns hauled down, pricked up a little and sent up again. Well, we lounged around the deck in all the panoply of grim-visaged war, all night, preceding and following more rockets, without results. It was a fraud. No tug came out to be gobbled, and we felt ill used. Just at daylight, or a little before, some one discov- a long, low black vessel about a mile distant, and every one was again all excitement and mystery. As it lightened, however, the vessel got larger, and we began to think that they had sent too big a tug for such a small schooner. As we stared at the vessel apprehensively, it growing bigger and bigger, a quartermaster, just behind me, muttered,

" If it ain't the Wabash, I'm a Dutchman."

Yes, we had been lying under the stern of the Wabash, flagship, all night, sending up rockets and showing green and red lights, to the great amuse-ment of the watchers on board that frigate.

RUM, PUNCH, OR BRANDY.

We hear so often of the free, open-hearted sailor, of his native simplicity and simple courage, that I know you will be glad of an instance in point relative to the qualities described.

An old boatswain's mate, learning that his former captain was in command of a ship lying off the navy yard, called to pay his respects; he was shown into the cabin, and the captain, unaffectedly glad to see his old shipmate, after a moment's conversation, said hospitably:

"Well, Jack, of course you'll have something to drink. Will you have some rum or some punch or a little brandy?"

"Thank ye, sir, much obliged," said the horny-handed son of the sea, with simple ingenuousness, "I think I will have a little rum while you're mixing the punch, and take the brandy afterward."

AN OLD TIME SPLENDID OFFICER.

I remember once, when a midshipman, while standing the mid-watch, I was gossiping with one of the quartermasters about the different officers in the service. I was much amused with the ideas of a splendid officer as entertained from the sailor's stand-point.

"There's Lieut. I——," said the quartermaster, "did you know him? I sailed with him in the

Levant; he was a *splendid* officer. I have seen him
come on deck to take the mid-watch so drunk that
he had to hold on to the bridge rail, and I have seen
him carry royals on her until he had the lee guns in
the water. I tell ye he was a *bully* officer. Why,
he'd put you in irons as soon as *look* at ye, he would;
he used to swear like a pirate when he was working
ship, and he was just as kind a man as you'd ever
want to sail with. Yes (with a sigh), he was just a
splendid officer."

I am glad to say however, that the *splendid* officers
above referred to are now very few and far between.

LAKE HURON IN JANUARY.

One cold winter on the lakes, a captain for a con-
sideration, agreed to bring a steamer from Chicago
to Detroit. While coming down Lake Huron, one
evening in January, the captain being on deck, beating his arms to try and keep from freezing to death,
he observed a man going forward with the red and
green sidelights, usually carried by vessels under-
weigh.

"What are you doing with those lights?" he
shouted.

"Going to put 'em on the bows."

"What for? Do you suppose that there is any
other infernal fool out, this time of year, but us?
Put 'em away."

LETTER XXI.

STATIONED AT NEWPORT — RECEIVING A FRENCH MAN-
OF-WAR — CONVERSATION UNDER DIFFICULTIES —
TELLING THE NEWS IN FRACTURED FRENCH — THE
ADMIRAL — GRAND CELEBRATION ON THE FOURTH
OF JULY — A BEAUTIFUL ILLUMINATION — AN INDE-
SCRIBABLE AND MAGNIFICENT DISPLAY — AN UN-
FORTUNATE INTERRUPTION AND CONSEQUENT LOSS
OF DIGNITY — A COLORED RESERVOIR OF FUN AND
MISCHIEF — TACKING SHIP BY BOOK.

Shortly after the capture of Richmond we were
lying at anchor off Newport, Rhode Island, when a
large French man-of-war came in and anchored near
us. As it was about 6 P. M our captain, fearing that
the Naval Academy authorities might not have
observed the arrival of the stranger, sent me on
board to welcome the new-comer and explain that the
hopitalities of the port would be extended, through
the proper officer, in the morning.

As I boarded the Frenchman, I said, slowly, to the
first officer that I met,

"DO YOU SPEAK ENGLISH, SIR?"

He extended his arms, raised his shoulders, bowed,
and passed me along to a second, with,

14

"*Entrez dans le cabin, Monsieur.*" (Enter the cabin, sir.)

I leisurely said to the second,

" Do you speak English, sir ? "

Following the precise example of his illustrious predecessor, he turned me over to a third. After the second repetition I said confidentially to the fourth,

" Surely *you* speak English, sir ? "

He bowed, extended his arms graciously, thereby raising his shoulders, and fairly entered me into the cabin.

I walked quickly up to a fine-looking officer, thinking, well, now *this is* the boss, and smiling sweetly, chanted my everlasting

" Do *you* speak English, sir ? "

He smiled, bowed, and extended his arms, thereby raising his shoulders (I think that I have used this expression before somewhere), and, turning to another good-looking Frenchman, presented me to the admiral in French.

I bowed pleasantly to the admiral, and drawing myself up haughtily, I gently whistled,

" Do you speak English, sir ? "

He smiled cheerfully, extended his arms, thereby raising his shoulders, bowed and said that he *didn't.* Feeling that I had touched bottom I sank into a chair and said:

"*Bong.*"

I then coolly,

announced who and what I was; told him that Newport was a place of baths; that the United States
Naval Academy was temporarily situated there; that
some one would be off in the morning to say how
d'ye do; that it was a very pleasant day, and what
ship is this, and where are you from. He answered
that it was the French line of battle ship "Jean
Bart," named after our celebrated French privateers-
man Jean Bart, you know (I said, "Oh, certainly"),
from Martinique.

While I was trying to remember whether Martinique was in the West Indies, or near Madagascar, east
coast of Africa, he continued in an easy (for him)
chat. in French, as to the weather they had had, etc.,
winding up by asking,

"What's the news?"

I answered,

"Oh, nothing in particular, but I have the latest
papers on board and will send them over when I
return to my own ship."

The admiral said then,

"Where is Sherman?"

"General Sherman? I don't know; perhaps in
Washington or maybe Chicago."

"Yes, but he made a great expedition."

"Oh, yes, a very great expedition."

"Yes, a big thing.   But where is he now?"

"Where?   I don't know exactly;   I guess in Washington."

"His army, where is it?"

I turned round and said:

"Look here, Monsieur, what is the last news you have had, anyway?"

He answered,

"March 1st."

TELLING THE NEWS.

"Didn't you know that Sherman marched to the sea; that he captured Savannah; that Richmond was taken; that Joe Johnston and Kirby Smith had surrendered?"

"Richmond was to be taken," he said, "but is not yet taken?"

"Well, it just *is* taken," said I.   "Didn't you know that the President had been assassinated?"

"What, Lincoln?"

"Yes, you see my sword hilt draped with crape, and my left arm with crape on!"

"Then Mr. Johnson is President now?"

"Yes, indeed."

"Oh, but that is terrible; the President assassinated; he was a good man, your Mr. Lincoln — how did it happen?"

Well, in my wretched French I told the sad story to my excited hearers, they rapidly supplying a word when I could not translate it. I told who Booth was, how he secreted himself near the box of the President at Ford's Theater, how he fired, leaped to the stage and escaped with a broken leg. How he was surrounded in a—a—(what is that place where you put horses?) *Ecurier*, thanks; how they said surrender. No, I fight till I die. How the bullet from John Boston Corbett's musket killed him, etc., until my mouth felt as if I had chewed gum for two hours steady.

Just then the cabin door opened and the orderly announced,

" *Un officier de la Marine des États Unis.*"

I jumped up saying,

"Here is

AN OFFICER FROM THE NAVAL ACADEMY.

I must step out."

As I moved towards the cabin door it opened again, and a lieutenant in the United States Navy came in, and walking up to me said hesitatingly,

" *Est ce que vous parlez Français?*"

" *Un peu,* Tom," said I—a little.

Poor old Tom, he was as blind as a bat, and couldn't tell me from a French admiral. Well, I rattled off what I knew, the ship's name, where from and what I had told them, and, exacting a promise not to tell ashore that I had been on board, I returned to my own ship.

The admiral came on board the Sabine before he sailed from Newport, and, on leaving, thanked me kindly for my information as above narrated.

Our officer of the deck spoke no French, but not relishing being left out of the conversation, would shout back in broken English answers to the questions as translated. It is funny, but it is the prevalent idea that when you wish a foreigner to understand you, you must talk abominable English to him, and drive it home by shouting.

We afterwards learned that the admiral spoke English tolerably well.

On the following

FOURTH OF JULY

we were lying in the harbor of New London, about half way between the Pequot House and the city. The captain had decided to illuminate the ship, in honor of the occasion, in grand style, so a liberal order for pyrotechnics was sent to Philadelphia, and we had on hand on the day in question enough sky-rockets, Roman candles and wheels, to blow the ship to—say Guinea.

We made all our arrangements to have the display come off at 10.30 P. M., and the programme was arranged with as much system and discipline as any evolution in seamanship would require.

At dusk, the men being all stationed and whips rove, the order was given,

"Lay aloft,"

"Trice up,"

and literally in a twinkling the ship was covered with lanterns, and presented the appearance of a great constellation.

I took a boat and pulled to one of the ships lying near in order to see how she looked.

The effect was

BEAUTIFUL IN THE EXTREME.

We had crossed top-gallant and royal yards for the purpose, and the lights at the fore, main and mizzen trucks, royal, top-gallant, topsail and lower yardarms, in the tops, at end of lower studding-sail, flying jib and spanker booms, at each cat-head, in each gangway, on each quarter, and at the peak, formed three beautiful arches of lights, with a great one at right angles traversing the three, and the ship—from stem to stern, from flying jib-boom up, over all the trucks, to the spanker boom.

At 10.30 P. M. the signal was given by the firing of a nine-inch gun and the men swarmed aloft, each man to a lantern; again, a second gun, and the fire-works began.

The royal yard men lighted red lights, the top-gallant yard men white and the topsail yard men blue, while the men at the lower yards burned all three at once.

The same order was observed on the head booms. In each gangway an immense wheel whizzed and flashed, while from the forecastle was sent up a rocket for each State.

The effect was

INDESCRIBABLE AND MAGNIFICENT

in the extreme. Throughout it all, order and discipline reigned; the pump brakes were shipped, the hose led along, buckets of water were filled and distributed all over the ship, and the sense of absolute security from fire, with the consciousness of perfect control should it take place, enhanced the pleasure of the scene. The fire-works being soon over, the *debris* was thrown into the convenient sea alongside, the pipes sounded the plaintive call for sweepers, and the decks being swept clean, the "pipe down" soon followed, and by 11.30 P. M. the profound stillness, broken only by the tread of the sentries and the officer of the deck, offered a striking contrast to the fiery, exciting scene of an hour before.

ENTERTAINING FRIENDS.

On one occasion, having been ordered as executive officer of a rather nice-looking steamer, I took the first opportunity that presented itself to invite some of my relatives to come on board and see the ship, and find out what an important individual I really was.

Shortly after the party came on board, I was summoned to the mast, by the officer of the deck, to hear a complaint against one of the crew, so turning my friends over to the care of one of the midshipmen. I repaired to the mainmast. Recognizing in the culprit an old offender, and the act a repetition of a former offense, and being irritated, also, by being called away from my friends, I was giving him fits, and telling him just what I was going to do with him, when I felt a hand on my shoulder, and an affectionate female voice say:

"KEEP YOUR TEMPER, FRANKIE.

Don't lose your temper my boy."

I felt the dignity of the man who had been executive officer of six or seven ships rock and sway: the scoundrel at the mast bit his lip to keep from smiling, and feeling that I could not do the subject justice, I fled from the sight of man—and woman.

Frequently after, when working ship, and giving some quick, short order, where promptness was absolutely necessary, I fancied that I could see the smile repeated on the faces of the crew and that they were muttering,

"Keep your temper, Frankie."

THE IRREPRESSIBLE DARKY,

alluded to in a former letter, used to try my patience very much.

Punishment seemed to roll off from his dusky hide like water. I have seen him stand on a capstan for hours and joke with some other offender near by, at the imminent risk, if detected by the officer of the deck, of being sentenced to four hours more.

Upon being asked after standing three hours on the topsail sheet bitts, what he was up there for, he replied, with a darkey chuckle,

"Lookin' out for whales, sir."

One night he was up for punishment, and was pacing the lee side of the quarter-deck; as he walked up and down, the spirit of mischief impelled him to give an extra slap on the deck with his bare foot as he turned to go forward; it is to be supposed that he presumed that the slap on the deck would disturb my slumbers, being applied just when he was nearest the window of my state-room looking out on deck.

I opened the blind, and said calmly,

"If it should happen that you unfortunately make that noise once more I shall be compelled to request the officer of the deck to station you on the capstan, where it won't be noticed."

For a time the fear of having to stand still until midnight on the capstan, instead of the freedom of the deck, deterred him, but not long; he couldn't stand it, and in less than ten minutes the *spat* of his big foot, just outside my window, was the forerunner of his transfer to the capstan, too far away for him to annoy me any more.

TACKING SHIP BY BOOK.

A midshipman being required to take the deck and tack ship, placed himself near the capstan, which concealed a copy of "Totten's Naval Text-Book."

At the order of "mainsail haul," the swing of the yards and heavy after sails turned over two pages of his book, unbeknownst to him, to the evolution of "bringing ship to an anchor," and he astonished all hands by promptly calling out the next order on the page, which happened to be,

"Let *go* the starboard anchor."

LETTER XXII.

"Sails were spread to ev'ry wind that blew,
    Raw were the sailors, and the depths were new."

A BATCH OF YARNS — FALLING FROM ALOFT — TWO
MIDSHIPMEN DISCOVER WHERE THE MIZZEN-TOP-
SAIL HALLIARDS ARE BELAYED — ONE WAY TO GET
"HOME ORDERS" — A COLLISION ON THE MISSIS-
SIPPI — HANGING JUDAS ISCARIOT — HOW TO MAKE
A SAILOR WORK — THE FRENCHMAN'S FAULT.

We were one day beating into the Capes of the
Chesapeake. The ship was under all plain sail —
courses, topsails, top-gallant sails, royals, jib, flying
jib and spanker — although it was blowing quite
fresh.

As we tacked, first to the northward, then to the
southward, the breeze freshening as we got in toward
the shore, the yards came round at the order, "mainsail haul," with great force, and it seemed as if the
heavy tack and sheet blocks would stave in the waist
boats at their davits.

LOSING A YARD.

On the last tack the helm was put down, the tack
raised, and at

" Haul taut," " mainsail haul,"

round came the main and cross-jack yards with a tremendous rush, and crash! went the mizzen top-gallant yard, carried away in the slings. We took in the mizzen-royal and top-gallant sail and sent down the yard for repairs. The yard was broken square in two, and there was nothing to do but to make a new one out of a spare spar, which was done so soon that it was up and across on the following day. I called the small boy to me, that was tending the mizzen top-gallant and royal braces, but he swore by all that he most valued, namely, his ration of duff, that he *did* let go the brace, and that it *didn't* jam in the block, so I had authentic information that the yard broke itself, and it is so recorded in the log book, the veracious history of our celebrated cruise.

FALLING FROM ALOFT.

Men and boys frequently fall from aloft, generally, however, from their own carelessness; they become used to moving about quickly, while aloft, and if permitted will run the most foolhardy risks.

I had to give a peremptory order, inflicting a severe penalty on any of the crew who should run out on the yards instead of by the foot ropes, which hang below the yard, enabling the person to hold on to the yard itself. At sea, no man is permitted to work outside the ship's rail unless he has a bowline round

him, with the end of the rope fast inboard, yet they
will do it, unless very carefully watched.

Midshipmen frequently fall from aloft, but being
warrant officers, they invariably escape serious injury.
I saw one fall from the main top-gallant yard, strike
on the topsail yard and bound down into the maintop, and he was all right again in two days; another
fell from the fore top-gallant yard, down about
twenty-five feet, on to the topsail yard, thence about
forty feet, striking the belly of the foresail, bounded
up, came down crosswise on a windsail bowline,
stretched across the forecastle, about ten feet above
the deck, and came down sitting, somewhat bewil-
dered, but not hurt; a third, just as he climbed on the
rim of the foretop, turned his foot on a small rope,
called the starboard fore top-gallant studding-sail
boom tricing line, fell striking his chin on the rim of
the top, breaking several back teeth, lit in the fore-
rigging on his back, rolled down the incline, bounded
over the rail, striking his head on one of the guns,
projecting from a gun-deck port, and into the water,
a distance entire of seventy-five feet. He was picked
up, and was able to be about in a few days, nearly as
good as new. If he had been anything but a midshipman he would have been killed three or four
times. A friend of mine on shore, who, unfortunately for him, was not one of those who "seldom die

and *never* resign," fell off his chair one day and broke his arm so badly that he had to have it taken off.

KILLING A FORE-YARD MAN.

A few days after, while at anchor in the Elizabeth River, off Norfolk, all hands were called for exercise in loosing and furling sail. The top-gallant and royal yard men had started first, followed by the topmen, and the orders had been given,

"Aloft, lower yard men,"

"Man the boom tricing lines,"

"Trice up."

The heavy topmast studding-sail booms, which lie on the fore-yard, when triced up, swing aft somewhat, as soon as they clear the yard, on account of the lead of the tricing line aft. The order being given,

"Lay out and loose,"

a number of fore-yard men laid out on the yard, and a young fellow about nineteen stepped upon the patent truss, at the same time looking aft and laughing at some one following him. Just then the heavy boom swung aft and struck him in the head. He fell some fifty feet and struck the man who was tending the tricing line, between the shoulders, then struck the fife-rail and dropped on deck. The foremast man, who was considerably hurt, let go the tricing line, and the heavy boom came down again, and pinned about a dozen boys, who were loosing sail, to the yard. It was very ludicrous for a moment, to see those little fellows jammed in under the boom with their arms and legs sticking out forward and aft, looking as if they were spitted like butterflies. There were so many of them, however, that no one was seriously hurt, and they could not fall because they were under the boom. The poor fellow that fell, however, was injured internally, and lived only twenty-four hours.

INSTRUCTING MIDSHIPMEN.

One day we were making sail, the topsails had been hoisted, and every one was flying around in answers to the quick, sharp orders of the officer of the deck.

"Let go the port mizzen topsail buntline," some one said, so Andy H——, a midshipman, anxious to do something, jumped aft and let go the mizzen topsail halliards. The yard came down with a run; the rope darted up in the air; Andy held on until he was about ten feet up, and then dropped on deck on his back, having lost most of the skin from his hands. But old Kirby K——, a sleepy, good-natured fat midshipman, who was standing in the port gangway, looking on amiably at the bustle around him, did not observe that his feet were in the bight of the

topsail halliards, which had not been coiled down
since the hoisting of the sail. When Andy let go
the rope, however, and his feet shot out from under
him, he sat down and wondered if the earthquake
had killed any more beside himself. Both Andy and
Kirby know now exactly where the mizzen topsail
halliards are belayed.

A SALUTE.

We were one day making preparations for firing a
salute, when a boat dashed alongside and an English
officer came on board. He introduced himself as the
commander of H. B. M. Styx, lying a few hundred
yards from us on our port beam.

He laughingly alluded to a quarrel between our
men and the crew of the English man-of-war Buz-
zard, and said, that seeing that we were about to
fire a salute, he thought it safe to call and ask that
we would take particular care that *all* the tompions
were removed from the guns before firing.

"Sailors will be sailors you know," he said, "and
as we are lying right under your guns, one or two of
those heavy tompions, left in, would make a hole in
us."

I have met a great number of English naval officers, and take great pleasure in saying that they are
invariably gentlemen.

15

A "MIDDY'S" RUSE.

An order came out to the commodore of the East India squadron to send all the forty date of midshipmen home for examination.

The word was passed for all the young gentlemen who had entered the service in 1840 to report on the quarter-deck. When the old commodore came out, and looked at the overjoyed youngsters, who were going home, he asked each one gruffly:

"Are you forty date, sir?"

"Are you sir?"

"You, sir?"

until he came to a midshipman who had entered two years later, and who was standing quite near the rest, who hesitatingly answered,

"I sir, I am forty-two, sir."

When the young gentleman reached the States, the Department showed some surprise that the commodore should have sent home one of the forty-two date, who had only been on the station a year.

DUCKING A RECUSANT.

A number of years ago, on board one of our large frigates, one of the men refused to do duty, "defying the whole caboodle of 'em to make him do anything." So the first lieutenant sent for one of the stout coal bags, and putting a couple of round shot in the bottom to give weight to the discipline, he had the unruly member placed in it, with his hands tied behind him, the bag being tightly laced around his throat, with his head out. Amid sarcastic remarks by the rebel, a line was bent on to the becket or handle, run through a block on the fore yard-arm, thence through a block in the slings of the yard, and being snatched was led along the deck. At the order, fifty men ran away with the line, and our hero was suddenly swung oscillating and vibrating to the fore yard-arm. As soon as he got his breath he railed at all hands, and abused everybody until he was tired. The mastman, watching his opportunity, suddenly threw off the turn, and down a clean drop of sixty feet, went the coal bag into the water. Away went the men again with a run (they enjoyed it as much as any one, and even more than the man in the bag), and dripping and puffing, up went the bag man to the yard-arm.

Still unsubdued, he swore and talked until he saw that no one paid any attention to him, and finally under the influence of the wetting and the hot sun, he got asleep. Off went the turn again, and down went the bag again, carried well under water by the friendly round shot, inside, and then up went the dripping victim to his station. When he got fairly up, and the horrible vibrations had somewhat ceased, he looked appealingly to the officer of the deck and said:

"May I be let down, sir?"

"Certainly," was the reply.

Up went a topman and bending a guy to the guy in the bag, he was tenderly landed on deck, and set at liberty, turning out afterwards one of the best men in the ship.

You must remember, my boy, that these occurred in the palmy days, and if an executive officer tried any such thing now, the erudite and better posted sailor would prefer charges against him as long as your arm, and which forwarded to the Navy Department might deprive the arm of the service of a valuable auxiliary.

THE FRENCHMAN'S FAULT.

While one of our frigates lay at Malta, in the Mediterranean, some of the crew, on liberty, got into a terrible fight with the crew of a French man-of-war.

The executive officer was holding an investigation at the mast, the following day, when the captain of the maintop came up, and offered the following explanation:

"You see, sir, it was all the Frenchman's fault, sir. Me, and the coxswain of the gig, and Jimmy Leggs, and the captain of the foretop, sir, was a walking

down the street, just as quiet as lambs, sir, when
along came some Frenchman from the *E*twoil. I
wanted to be civil, so I says to 'em,

"'Will you come in and take a drink? says I.'

"'Kay?' says he.

"'Kay?' says Jimmy Leggs, 'what kind of an
answer is *that* to give a gentleman?'

and he up and hit him; and that's the way the row
began, sir. You see, sir, it were all the Frenchman's
fault, sir."

LETTER XXIII.

"Come, seize your glasses, fellows,
  And sit down in a ring;
For 'tis about this Naval School,
  That I'm about to sing.
You've oft heard tell of middies?
  God bless the young heroes!
And if half of them do not 'bilge,
  They'll be a terror to their foes.

U. S. NAVAL ACADEMY — HOW TO OBTAIN AN APPOINT-
MENT — QUALIFICATIONS FOR ADMISSION—PAY AND
EXPENSES — DESCRIPTION OF THE ACADEMY — THE
DAILY ROUTINE.

For the benefit of the aspirants for future naval
honors, I give a brief synopsis of the only method of
entering the navy of the United States as an officer.
All regular line officers of the navy must be graduates of the United States Naval Academy, now situated at Annapolis, Maryland.

NOMINATION.

The number of cadet-midshipmen allowed at the
Academy is one for every member and delegate of
the House of Representatives; one for the District
of Columbia, and ten appointed annually at large.

The nomination of candidates for admission from
the District of Columbia and at large is made by the
President. The nomination of a candidate from any

Congressional district or territory is made on the recommendation of the member or delegate from actual residents of his district or territory.

Each year, as soon after the 5th of March as possible, members and delegates will be notified in writing of vacancies that may exist in their districts. If such members or delegates neglect to recommend candidates by the first of July in that year. the Secretary of the Navy is required by law to fill the vacancies existing in districts actually represented in Congress. They will be filled by appointments from the districts in which the vacancies exist.

The nomination of candidates is made annually between the 5th of March and the 1st of July. Candidates who are nominated in time to enable them to reach the academy on the 21st of June will receive permission to present themselves at that time to the Superintendent of the Naval Academy for examination as to their qualifications for admission. Those who are nominated prior to July 1st, but not in time to attend the June examination, will be examined on the 12th of September following; and should any candidate fail to report, or be found physically or mentally disqualified for admission in June, the member or delegate from whose district he was nominated will be notified to recommend another candidate, who shall be examined on the 12th of September following. When any of the dates assigned for examinations fall on Sunday, the examination will take place on the following Monday.

A sound body and healthy constitution, good mental abilities, a natural aptitude for study and habits of application, persistent effort, an obedient and orderly disposition, and correct moral principles and deportment, are so necessary to success in pursuing the course at the academy, that persons conscious of deficiency in these respects are earnestly recommended not to subject themselves or their friends to the mortification and disappointment consequent upon failure, by accepting nominations and attempting to enter a service for which they are not fitted.

EXAMINATION.

Each candidate for appointment as cadet-midshipman must present to the Academic Board satisfactory testimonials of good moral character, and must certify on honor to his precise age, which must be over fourteen and less than eighteen years at the time of the examination. No candidate will be examined whose age does not fall within the prescribed limits.

Candidates must be physically sound, well formed, and of robust constitution; they will be required to pass a satisfactory examination before a medical board composed of one of the medical officers of the

Naval Academy and two other medical officers to be designated by the Secretary of the Navy.

ADMISSION.

Candidates who pass the physical and mental examinations will receive appointments as cadet-midshipmen and become inmates of the academy. Each cadet will be required to sign articles by which he binds himself to serve in the United States navy eight years (including his time of probation at the Naval Academy), unless sooner discharged. The pay of a cadet-midshipman is $500 a year, commencing at the date of his admission.

Each cadet-midshipman must, on admission, deposit with the paymaster the sum of $50, for which he will be credited on the books of that officer, to be expended, by direction of the superintendent, in the purchase of text-books and other authorized articles.

All the deposits for clothing, and the entrance-deposit of $50 must be made before a candidate can be received into the academy.

SUMMARY OF EXPENSES.

Deposit for clothing,	$169 70
Deposit for books, etc.,	50 00
Total deposit required,	$219 70

The value of clothing brought from home is to be deducted from this amount.

Each cadet-midshipmen, one month after admission, will be credited with the amount of his actual expenses in traveling from his home to the academy.

A cadet-midshipman, who voluntarily resigns his appointment within a year of the time of his admission to the academy, will be required to refund the amount paid him for traveling expenses.

THE ACADEMY

is delightfully situated, with the City of Annapolis on two sides and the Severn River and Chesapeake Bay on the other two.

The grounds are inclosed or separated from the city by a high brick wall with two gates, and midshipmen cannot pass beyond the limits of the academy except by written permission.

The midshipmen live in quarters, the different classes being as much as practicable together.

The Superintendent of the Aacademy is a naval officer of high rank, and the supervision and instruction of the cadets is, as much as practicable, directly by naval officers.

There is an academic examination in February, the academic year beginning October 1, and the regular annual examination in June of each year for each class, at which a board of visitors, appointed by the President of the United States, is present.

A graduate of the Naval Academy will have had thorough instruction in mathematics as high as trigonometry, analytical geometry and conic sections; in seamanship, naval construction, naval tactics, gunnery, infantry tactics, field artillery and mortar practice, fencing, steam engineering, astronomy, navigation and surveying, physics and chemistry, mechanics, law, history, drawing, French and Spanish: and he will not get through the various examinations in these branches unless he is thoroughly posted in each. I am happy to say that a Michigan representative took a single number last year, graduating No. 5 in a class of 45.

The academy grounds are very delightfully laid out with walks and fountains, boat-houses, with numerous boats to be used under reasonable restrictions, gymnasium, fencing and dancing hall, and a fine band; and is altogether a very enjoyable place to obtain a first-class education.

THE DAILY ROUTINE

is as follows:

Reveille, 6 A. M.

Roll-call and chapel, 6.45 A. M.

Breakfast, 7 A. M.

Sick call, 7.30 A. M.

Bugle call to studies, 7.56 A. M.

Bugle call for first recitation, 8.26 A. M.

Bugle call for second recitation, 9.26 A. M.

Bugle call for third recitation, 10.41 A. M.

Bugle call for fourth recitation, 11.41 A. M.

Drum dinner call, 12.55 P. M.

Bugle call for first afternoon recitation, 1.56 P. M.

Bugle call for second afternoon recitation, 2.56 P. M.

Bugle call to drill, 4.05 P. M.

Bugle recall for drill, 5.15 P. M.

Drum evening roll-call and parade, then supper, 6.30 P. M.

Drum call for gymnastic exercises, 15 minutes after supper.

Bugle call to evening studies, 7.30 P. M.

Gun fire and tattoo, 9.30 P. M.

Taps, 10 P. M.

On Sundays the programme is somewhat different, there being no recitations or drills. On Saturday there is a drill in the forenoon at great guns, naval tactics, or howitzer, or something of that kind, the remainder of the day and evening being for recreation.

The junior class entering in September goes to sea in June, after the examination, for a practice cruise until October 1. The following June they go on a leave of absence for the same time; going to sea for the second time in the June following, and graduating a year from that time, in June, as midshipmen, after a course of four years.

I see, however, by the last reports, that the Super-intendent of the Naval Academy recommends that for the present a fewer number of midshipmen and engineers be graduated from the academy, as with our few ships and small navy the supply is greater than the demand. Consequently the prospect is that an officer will attain middle life before reaching even a medium rank in the service.

LETTER XXIV.

REMINISCENCES OF THE OLD NAVAL ACADEMY — MEET-
ING A CLASSMATE BRINGS BACK "THE BOYS" TO
MEMORY — THE PRANKS OF MISCHIEVOUS MIDSHIP-
MEN REPEATED FOR THE BENEFIT OF THEIR CHIL-
DREN — A PLEASANT MEMORY OF CUSHING OF THE
ALBEMARLE — MUSICAL CULTURE OF THE SECOND
CLASS — PET NAMES FOR PRETTY BOYS — ORIGINAL
EXERCISES WITH A LIGHT BATTERY — BRICKS AS
AMMUNITION.

I met an old classmate the other day, and we
talked about

THE OLD NAVAL ACADEMY

all the evening. There were lots of names that I
had almost forgotten, but the train of conversation
brought them all up, even to their initials.

You remember Harrison; he was from Vir-
ginia, and went south during the war. You remember how he threw a brick at the watchman's lantern
and smashed it, and was so sound asleep when Johnny
M—— came round to inspect that he couldn't be
waked up, and how poor old W——n up stairs, who
was safe in bed, as he thought, after being "out on
French," was made to walk a seam, and failing

ignominiously, was suspended for being tight? "Attention to orders. Acting Midshipman Charles H. W——n is hereby placed under suspension for violation of article 7 of the United States Naval Academy regulations — intoxication. He will, therefore, while thus under suspension, govern himself in strict accordance with article 39, chapter 11 of the regulations established by the Navy Department. L. M. Goldsborough, Superintendent."

OLD GRISWOLD.

You remember Griswold, George H.; he was from Detroit; he roomed with Gregory, of New York. Gregory shaved Griswold's eyebrows off one evening while he was asleep, and he did look like thunder. Gregory used to play the organ in the chapel, and would "wander by the brookside" in the voluntary until some professor's attention was called to it, when he would tone down in a hymn.

Griswold afterwards roomed v' ohnny Northrop, from South Carolina; h ook John's pillow-case off one evening to get shell oysters in, and the ever-patient John got mad and licked him for it.

Griswold and Gregory came out of dinner one day and went into Sanderson's room, in No. 3 building (Sanderson was a tall, lanky fellow from Pennsylvania), and tilted the table up against the door and piled mattress, wash-bowl and pitcher, looking-glass and bottle of ink on top of everything, so when old Sanderson burst into his room it would all come down, and Sanderson was spotted next day for "ink on floor," and got six demerits.

You know 200 demerits, in one year, would dismiss you. You remember Gregory got 580 before the February examination. The daily report of conduct at evening parade used to read: Gregory, visiting in study hours, 10; the same, the same, 10; the same, untidy room, bed not made at morning inspection, 6; the same, inattentive at drill, 4; the same, absent from 8 A. M. recitation, 6; the same, skylarking during study hours, etc.; Robinson, C. H., skulking from drill.

THERE WAS DICK PRENTISS, POOR FELLOW,

he was killed at Mobile. Dick taught us how to blow the gas out in the rest of the building, by putting your handkerchief over the burner and blowing in the pipe until you were black in the face; and how to rig tin water pails over the door so as to duck the officer in charge when he came round and opened the door.

Dick and another fellow were down on the wharf one day, and the other fellow said he would jump in if Dick would, so Dick jumped in over his head, and then the other fellow wouldn't jump.

You remember Cushing, of the Albemarle, and I had a fight behind the battery one evening, and Cushing—no—I, got thrashed?

BOOTS.

Old John Taylor Wood came round inspecting one day, and Shute (you remember Francis Asbury Shute, of Mulliky Hill, New Jersey) had put a pair of boots artistically under his bed, and pulled the spread down so you could just see them. So old John said, gruffly,

"Visiting in study hours, eh? Come out."

And when he didn't come out, he pulled at the boots, which readily came out, colored crimson and went out. The next day you could see artistic boots in nearly every room in No. 1 building, and an order came out, "that the bed spread should be tucked in under the mattress, so a clear view of the floor could be had."

THE SECOND CLASS GOT A HAND-ORGAN,

and used to serenade everybody in the yard, until one day a fellow was playing during study hours, in a window on the third floor of No. 4 building, when a watchman came to the room and said,

"That the officer in charge had sent down for that organ."

"This organ?" said the midshipman, giving it a

16

careless nudge with his elbow, "why certainly," and the watchman gathered up the pieces of pipe on the pavement thirty feet below, or what was left of them. The superintendent of the building got spotted, however, for neglect of duty in permitting an organ to be played during study hours.

YOU REMEMBER "KATY."

The midshipmen called him Katy because he had such red cheeks and was so pretty. Tom Mills used to say,

"Katy, you dear old girl, come here and give me a kiss and stop beating the drum."

Katy was knock-kneed a little, which, in sailor parlance, was called beating the drum. There was "Fanny" Spencer — he's dead now, poor fellow; "Martha" Dickens, "Sophy" Swan, "Polly" White, "Nancy" Blue, all pretty boys. They have grown up into bearded officers with little trace of their former red cheeks.

Old C. S. Hunt; he got very much excited on religion, Darwinism, and resigned. He said he had saved up enough money when he "went on leave," to pay his fare home and back and give "Yank R—— ginger snaps all the way." Yank is a commander now, and a very good one, I hear.

"DUNKER" A.

You remember the day we were all down to recitation in electricity with Hopkins, and we all formed a line round a Leyden jar, and Dunk touched the knob and seemed to be fearfully overcome with the shock, kicked over the jar and rolled over and over on the floor, until old Hopkins laughed himself hoarse, saying, that he never saw it affect any one so before.

Dunk was attached to the academy afterward, at Newport, as a lieutenant, and on his first day's duty at the Atlantic House, the watchman came in and reported that the lower sash of room No. 26 was raised. Dunk said at once:

"Will you please tell me what in thunder I care whether the lower sash is raised or not?"

So I had to explain that the lower lights of glass are painted and are not to be raised during study hours, so the attention of the midshipman shall not be taken from his studies.

"KA-NIPE."

Do you remember old Ka-nipe? He used to cut his tobacco in so many pieces and put himself on an allowance of so many chews a day, and when he was on the pledge not to use tobacco in the academy grounds, he went out on Long Wharf and stuck a plank out over the Severn River and sat on the end of it, so as to be outside the academy limits, and chewed and spit into the river.

ECCENTRIC ARTILLERY DRILL.

Do you remember the evening we took the park of light artillery all to pieces, and dismounted the guns, and run the wheels in all directions, and threw the linch pins into the river? Old Jas. I. Waddell was officer in charge. (Jas. I. commanded the rebel Shenandoah afterward during the war.) Wasn't he mad? McGonegal said that it was lucky for him that *he* wasn't in charge, or he would have been detached from the academy, sure.

There was Nick Stanton and Doolittle who roomed together. Nick jumped out of the second story of No. 3 building one evening, because he would not be dared, and it never hurt him a bit.

PRESENCE OF MIND.

There were two fellows in No. 3 building "went on French" out in town one night, and got full of rum. Well, one of them got caught, and the doctor came down and gave him some ammonia that sobered him instantly, and the other fellow said that was a good thing to have, and stole the bottle. He got caught afterwards, putting bricks in the guns at light artillery drill, just to see 'em skip across the bay to the detriment of passing schooners.

A RETORT.

One year the Wabash came there with Franklin
Pierce on board, and a British man-of-war, the Cura-
çoa, to take Lord Napier home; a little son of Lord
Napier said to a young midshipman in the boat,
going off to the ship,

"I suppose those stripes on your flag are the ones
you put on the backs of your slaves, ain't they?"

"Yes," said the middy, "and those are the stars
we made you see at Bunker Hill."

There was Jacobs, W. C.; he resigned when a second class man, and now is a doctor out in Ohio with
the income of a commodore.

You remember old DeBree, first lieutenant of the
practice ship Plymouth?

One day the midshipmen were exercising on the
fore yard, shrieking and making an awful noise; poor
old Simon couldn't hear at all, but he thought, by the
looks, that they were raising thunder, so he turned to
me and said nervously,

"Ain't they talking *some* up there?"

"Yes, sir, particularly in the slings,"
so he hailed them to make less noise in the slings.

You remember Woodhull Smith Schenck? Well,
old Schenck went out to Japan after he resigned, and
is now a rich man.

Jimmy Tayloe was killed on board the rebel ram

Merrimac. Bull Carnes commanded a rebel howitzer battery in Tennessee.

Averett and Dornin were on board the privateer Florida. Armstrong was on the Alabama.

Savez Read was the pirate of the Taconey that cut the Caleb Cushing out of Portland, and afterward ran the C. H. Webb down the Mississippi. Read was leader of the second section in French, and when marching to recitation used to look back and say,

"Catch pied, now you fellows,"

for catch step, and as he always said,

"Savez?"

for "do you understand?" they always called him Savez Read.

You remember how ten fellows were dismissed for tarring and feathering Foote, of my class, and the midshipman had a court of inquiry to find out exactly who did it?

Tom Fister, of Berks County, Penn; he seceded during the war, had been bragging of how much he had done, until he found that they were to be punished for it when he became as innocent as a dove.

Savez Read was president of the court, and he cross-examined Tom somewhat as follows:

"You didn't hang out of your window for two hours with a d——d big rope with a running noose in it to catch Foote when he came by?"

"No, sir."

"You didn't run round the rear of building No. 3 with a pail of tar crying, 'Come on fellows, we've got him,' did you?"

"No, sir, I was only running down to the gas house to see what they was going to do with him."

The evidence being too strong, Tom was convicted and all ten were dismissed. They went up to Washington, however, and after being the lions for a week, were re-instated in their own class.

You know Jug M—— committed suicide out in China. Zimmerman was blown up in the Westfield off Galveston.

Charley Swasey was killed on board the Scioto, and there is only half a dozen left out of a class that had altogether 116 in it. Well, twenty-two years make great changes, and, my boy, we are getting along in years though we don't realize it.

Old Don Roget, he was professor of Spanish; when we came to the sentence in Ollendorf,

"Have I the horse that you have?"
each class, every year, used to insist on an explanation, resulting somewhat as follows:

"One ting cannot be in two places at the same time, except it be a bird that can fly very quick; two tings cannot be in the same place at the same time, unless there be room for both of dose tings; two per-

sons cannot sit in the same chair, at the same time,
unless de chair be wide enough for both of dose persons; true, one might sit in de oder's lap, but dat is
not it."

"You will now proceed after de explanation."

He hated musk, and the midshipmen used to go up
with high standing collars, all scented with musk,
and he would have to dismiss the class and air the
room.

One day "Savez" Read carried up a Lubin bottle
filled with sulphuretted hydrogen, and while vainly
trying to get the glass stopper out, he dropped it on
the floor and it rolled to the middle of the room;
of course everybody laughed. Don said,

"Mr. Read, I will report you for making a laugh."

"I didn't make a laugh."

"You dropped dat bottle."

"Yes, but I didn't go to do it."

"Did you drop dat bottle to make a laugh or did
you not?"

"I did not."

"Very well, I will report somebody. Mr. Hoag
I'll report you because you laughed *first*, and Mr.
Schley, I'll report you because you laughed *loudest;* I
am never tired of making reports,"
and he *did*. Pinkey Hoag turned even pinker with
restrained laughter, but got six demerits just the

same. He told Ned Furber that those French poo-
dles would be Creoles if born in the United States.

I never shall forget Mug Foster; they called him
Mug because he always had a sore lip. He was at
the academy eighteen months, and he always had a
boil on his upper lip that swelled his face up and
made him unhappy. He roomed with Adj. Wharton
when a fourth class man. Wharton got his name
from Foster's telling how he used to make him
march up and down the room while he gave the
orders as he would if he were adjutant,

"Fust captains to the front and centah — mawch."

"Front,"

"Repawt,"

"Posts,"

"Mawch."

The best of the joke was, that Wharton was both
adjutant and subadjutant of first and second class,
being a very smart fellow, and would have been a
credit to the service if he had not chosen to go
south with his state. Sardine Graham, S., was a
smart fellow too, and stood two in the class. Old
Sardine is a clerk of court in Alabama, I think,
with seven children all the same size.

Do you remember how old John W—— used to
sneak round in rubbers to catch us visiting or smoking? and how old Billy M—— skipped upstairs like

any midshipman, and then came down, scooping 'em all very much, like any officer in charge?

They used to say that John Taylor Wood would come into a building and tap on the steam pipes, to indicate an officer coming, and then wait for a few minutes so as to give them all a chance to be ready for inspection. I think that we were better behaved for being treated decently, don't you?

Those bugle calls to recitation and study hours, I can whistle them as readily as I could twenty years ago. You remember how some of our class spiked the morning gun so that they couldn't fire it for reveille.

Count Segur was professor of fencing and drawing while we were fourth class,

" Get on, young gentlemen, get on."

I used to get him talking and he would tell stories and draw almost all of my picture. What stories he used to tell, and how he used to exaggerate them:

" Young gentlemen, one day I was riding on a mule on the Isthmus of Panama, and had stood up in order to make a sketch; I suddenly caught a view of both oceans, a thing never before seen, I was sketching rapidly when my mule started, and I was suspended by my eyelids over a frightful precipice; I never lost my presence of mind, however, and completed my sketch before I came down. Get on."

I remember when I was in the fourth class, that Lockwood, who was professor of infantry tactics, had a good deal of trouble in teaching us the first rudiments of the drill. He knew only one of us by name, and when he saw a fellow inattentive he would promptly call out,

" Ha-a re-e-port Mr. Spencer-a-a-inattentive on drill."

" My name isn't Spencer, sir."

" Oh, a-ha where *is* Mr. Spencer,"
and Spencer was looked up and spotted just the same.

Poor old Bab, he's out west book-keeping, for some one in a tobacco house, he having sympathized on the wrong side in the " late unpleasantness."

Lockwood was professor of natural philosophy when I was in the first class. I remember, one day, he had just finished an experiment for the first section, when the second section came in (of course, I was in the second section, there being but two in the class), and I quietly took the wine-glass, filled with spirits of wine and covered with a piece of bladder, out of the bowl of water, pricked it and let it squirt under the table without Lockwood seeing me. When it came time to exhibit the experiment the professor took the wine-glass from the water, and commenced,

" You-a-a-see that this wine-glass is filled with spirits of wine, covered with bladder, and has been immersed in water; the water having less attraction for the bladder than the spirits of wine, it will force itself into the glass and distend the bladder, making the surface convex; if now I prick the bladder, a jet will ensue."

Well, he pricked the bladder, and there was no jet, of course. Turning, he fixed his eye on me and said hesitatingly and angrily,

" Di–i–d yo–o–ou prick tha–a–at ? "

" Yes, sir."

" Well, I wish that you wouldn't fool with these experiments any more. Gentlemen the section is dismissed."

And now that I have got back to my *alma mater*, the dear old academy from which I started out so full of life and hope, seventeen years ago, having passed through many varied and exciting scenes, yet accomplishing so little of what I had hoped, it seems fitting that I should close these sketches here. To those who have followed me through them all, I thank you heartily; pleased, if I have been able to contribute to your amusement, if you are a sailor, or if I have added to your store of information as regards a " Man-of-War," if a landsman.

To those who would be critical, I ask their indulgence, with the plea that I never wrote a book before, and I will never, *never* do it again.

Since 1870, when I retired from active service, the fashion of naval things has changed as materially as have others. A Phonograph, on the bridge, will recite the orders for tacking and working ship without making a mistake, and never turn over two leaves at once; Torpedoes, and improved Gatling guns, Rams and sub-marine engines of destruction, have taken the place of the weapons with which I am familiar; and should adverse fate, and the order of the President, send me once more to sea, I should not only have to learn much that is new, but unlearn many of the old-fashioned notions I have just imposed upon a confiding public—as the latest out.

www.ingramcontent.com/pod-product-compliance
Lightning Source LLC
Chambersburg PA
CBHW030804020726
47499CB00006B/1761